# Doors & Windows
## A Liam & Jonah Novella

# A.J. BARLOWE

# DOORS & WINDOWS

*a Liam & Jonah novella*

*Doors & Windows* is a follow-up story to the novel *A Series of Rooms* and is not intended to be read as a standalone.

CONTENT WARNING:
This novella includes references to past sexual assault and is largely a story about someone learning how to live and thrive after experiencing trauma.

For M.

*I hope this makes you think of summer '19.*

# CHAPTER 1
# Liam

The box hit the top of the second staircase with a crash that sounded a lot like structural damage. Liam Cassidy shook out his bloodless fingers, striped with indents from the sharp edges of cardboard, and leaned back against the wall to catch his breath.

It was the sweltering armpit of August in New York City, and even his proverbial rose-colored glasses were starting to fog up inside this stairwell.

In most of Liam's daydreams about life in the city, air conditioning was a factor he took for granted. Perhaps an elevator was, too.

His new apartment building was old. The exterior fit the aesthetic that every wannabe-struggling-artist wanted for their first place in New York. Aged brick had been patched over through the years with coloring that didn't quite match all the way down, the entry door was layered in spray paint that hadn't been scrubbed away since the Reagan administration, and a set of Oscar the Grouch-style trash cans lined the sidewalk.

The interior reflected much more practical concerns. The stairs didn't so much *creak* as they did buckle under the slightest movement. The painted walls of the hallways were scratched with jagged, overlapping stripes, evidence of a decade's worth of furniture moving in and out of the building. Now Liam was making his own contribution to the disarray. There was something magical about that, right?

Maybe his rose-colored glasses hadn't dimmed so much after all.

At the sound of footsteps behind him—frankly impossible to miss, with the way the entire staircase shook—Liam nudged the box closer to the wall with his foot, clearing a path.

Jonah Prince turned the corner with a duffle bag slung over one shoulder and a bag of Liam's bedding hoisted onto the other. The sight of him standing there in the flesh, mere meters between them instead of hundreds of miles, still took his breath away. Liam hadn't quite righted his equilibrium since he first lay eyes on Jonah that morning, standing on the sidewalk outside his new apartment, holding two coffee cups and Liam's entire heart in his hands.

His hair was longer now. After eight months of watching the progression over video calls, Liam still wasn't used to seeing the growth in person: brown-black waves that curled over the tips of his ears and at the nape of his neck, currently clinging to his forehead in sweaty tendrils, which was far more appealing than it had any right to be.

Liam's own exertion probably just made him look like he was melting.

"Taking a break?" Jonah's voice was unfairly steady. Liam's, on the other hand, was strained between pulls for oxygen.

"There's a reason I'm sticking to the arts," he said. "Manual labor is not for everyone. We didn't all spend our summers throwing around steel beams for fun."

Jonah's laugh filled the stairwell, still a rare enough delight that Liam had to clutch the wobbly railing behind him.

"I did offer to carry that one for you," Jonah pointed out, nodding to the box on the landing. He had yet to put down either of the heavy bags in his arms.

"Yeah," Liam said, "but it feels like kind of a dick move to bring my entire home library to college and make someone else carry it up four flights of stairs."

"Only two flights now." Jonah tilted his head toward the next set. "Trade me?"

"Are you sure?" Liam asked.

But Jonah was already moving, stepping around him to drop the bags on the landing. He crouched in front of the box and lifted it with practiced ease.

And Liam's mind just sort of... blanked.

Because there was Jonah, with his sweat-damp hair and his kind gestures and his short sleeves that strained around his upper arms when they flexed against the weight. With his well-worn boots from a long summer of construction work braced on the wooden steps and the movement of his back muscles when he tossed a look back at him. And Liam was so in love he couldn't think straight.

"You coming?" Jonah asked.

Liam closed his mouth and swallowed, his throat suddenly dry for reasons entirely unrelated to the heat. "Yeah," he said. "Right behind you."

When the final box was unloaded, Liam collapsed onto the bare mattress, currently situated on the floor in the corner of his closet-sized bedroom.

Jonah hovered in the scant patch of open floor, glancing quickly toward the spot beside Liam before settling onto the window ledge instead. He pulled two bottles of water from his backpack and handed one to Liam, who downed half in one messy, dribbling go. It wasn't like anyone could tell the water stains apart from all the sweat on his shirt, anyway.

"Better?" Jonah asked.

"Ask me again when I've had a shower." Liam grimaced, lifting the hem to wipe his forehead. He meant to continue that thought, but when he dropped the material from his eyes, he caught a fleeting glimpse of Jonah looking away from his exposed stomach.

A history of poor self-esteem might have made him self-conscious in any other context. But this was Jonah, the boy who brought out a whole new spectrum of emotions in Liam, so that feeling low in his belly was something else. Something warm and languid. Something like the urge to make Jonah want to look at him like that again.

It wasn't new, this sparkling desire between them, but it wasn't exactly familiar either. In Chicago, their shared experience with physical intimacy had been limited. Outside of the one reckless, perfect, catastrophic night in Liam's childhood bedroom, the timing had never felt right. Liam was always cognizant of Jonah's circumstances and the power dynamic it created between them.

It had been eight months since everything changed. The recovery wasn't so cut-and-dry; the things that Jonah had been subjected to couldn't be undone, and the scars he was left with wouldn't suddenly disappear with a change of scenery. But slowly, gradually, Liam had watched the heaviness recede from Jonah's features, new life creeping in from the edges.

The spring and early summer had seen a shift between them. In their nightly calls, their conversations began to take the occasional turn into something flirtatious, something more. In one particular instance, the slow sizzle had built to a peak, both of their voices breathy and thick as Liam's fingers dipped below the waistband of his sweatpants.

(That was not something he needed to be thinking about right now).

Liam cleared his throat at the same time Jonah found something interesting to look at out the window.

With either the best or worst timing, a man roughly Liam's own age appeared in the bedroom doorway—tall and lean, wearing a Fordham Athletics shirt with a duffle bag thrown over one shoulder.

"Oh, hey." The hint of a valley accent made Liam picture him on a surfboard somewhere in California. "You must be Liam."

A sense of unease crept in before he could quash it, dampening the edges of his good mood even more than the humidity. It was unfair of Liam to make a personal judgment at a glance, but he couldn't help reacting to the fact that his new roommate looked like he could have been the evil triplet of his shitty ex-friends, Nathan and Ben.

Rooming with strangers from an online student forum had been a gamble, but one that came with an appealing price tag and at least the potential for common ground with his roommates. But if this guy's first impression was true to form, Liam didn't know if he could take another year of mean-spirited jokes and sports references and casual homophobia.

He forced a smile up at him anyway. "Yep, that's me. You're... Tucker?"

"Hell yeah. Nice to meet you, dude." Tucker stepped into the room, dropping his bag at the door and bounding toward him with an outstretched hand. Liam stared at it a moment too long before he realized that he was offering a hand up. He tentatively took it and nearly toppled over from the strength of the grip that pulled him up.

"Bring it in, man!"

Before Liam could process that, he was scooped into an enthusiastic hug that took his feet off the ground. His eyes widened over Tucker's shoulder and found Jonah watching the exchange, brows lifted.

Maybe Liam was the only asshole here.

"Welcome to the penthouse!" Tucker released him with a final clap to his shoulder. "Sorry I wasn't here to help you haul stuff up—Izzy already staked a claim on my muscle this morning."

Isabel, the second roommate in question, trailed in behind him. She was the visual ideal of every New York art student: two long braids tucked back under a bandana, a silver ring through her septum, and sporadic tattoos up the length of both arms. She wore a pair of paint-splattered overalls and the kind of easy confidence Liam could never pull off.

He desperately wanted her to like him.

She shot Tucker a withering look, then turned a smile on Liam. "Hey there. Glad you got in okay with the spare key," she said. "Bad timing—I had Tucker booked this morning before I knew you'd be moving in. It occasionally boosts his ego to model for my summer acrylic class. It's Liam, right?" Her hand, when she reached out to bump his fist, was smudged with flecks of dried paint. "I'm Izzy."

"Yeah, hi." Liam tapped his knuckles against hers. "No worries. It was quick work between the two of us. Mostly him." He gestured back to Jonah, who stood from his perch. "This is my..." He stopped, voice sticking in his throat. "Um, this is Jonah."

*Real smooth, Cassidy.*

If Jonah noticed his flub, he took mercy on him and ignored it, nodding a polite greeting at Liam's new roommates. For a moment, Liam worried that Tucker would try to repeat his bear hug on Jonah, who still struggled with strangers in his personal space on the best of days, but Tucker kept it to a polite wave.

Izzy glanced between them, appraising. "Will we be seeing a lot of you around here, Jonah?" she asked. "Or are you hired muscle as well?"

Liam stiffened, but Jonah just let out a quiet huff, glancing at Liam and raising a brow. "As long as Liam decides to keep me around," he said.

Liam was disproportionately happy with that answer. He smiled and added with absolute certainty, "That's a yes."

■■■■■■■■■■■■■■■■■■■■■■■■■■■■■■■■■■■■■■■■■■■■■■■■■

Five stories of distance did little to dampen the noise of Amsterdam Avenue, but the ambience was a comfort. It cradled Liam and Jonah where they nestled together on the fire escape, two cartons of lo mein and orange chicken propped on the oversized book they were using as a table. The sky was an endless golden-pink at the close of sunset, and Liam wished he hadn't left his phone inside. He wanted to capture the image of a perfect evening and see if he could do justice to the scene in paint later.

"Thank you," Liam said after a stretch of comfortable, exhausted quiet. "It means a lot that you took the day off to help me move."

It had been a bit of a back-and-forth with his parents, the decision to drive to New York on his own. The belongings he brought with him were just enough to fill a midsize rental car (he had sold his own before moving to give himself a nest egg of cash), but it meant there was no room for passengers. His mom had offered to fly in and meet him to help get him settled, but Liam had finally succeeded in assuring her that he and Jonah could handle it.

Aside from the logistics just making more sense, the solo road trip had also been appropriately commemorative of his journey into independence. He'd gotten through an entire audiobook, plus part of a playlist he had curated specifically for the drive. And now, exhausted and sweaty but stupidly content, Liam was glad that it was just the two of them here to bask in the afterglow.

"I wouldn't have missed it," Jonah said.

Liam tamped down on the rollercoaster-drop in his stomach and bumped his shoulder. "Were you excited to see me or something?"

"Nah." Jonah bumped him back. "It's not like we had a running countdown or anything."

He was so beautiful in this light. Jonah was beautiful in every light—rooftop moonlight, hotel lamplight, hospital fluorescents—but in the golden hour, he glowed. Liam openly watched him, Jonah dutifully pretending he didn't notice as he busied himself with another bite of noodles from the carton. He couldn't believe he was here with him. He couldn't believe that his luck had unfolded so uncharacteristically, giving him the two things he wanted more than anything: New York and Jonah, tied together with a ribbon.

He had to squeeze his fingers around the pocked iron rung of the fire escape to keep himself from reaching out and touching his hair. It was such a new part of Jonah; one that represented freedom and autonomy and a fresh start. Liam counted himself lucky for the chance to fall in love with his image all over again.

"I'm still not used to seeing it like this," Liam said, letting his eyes graze over the growth.

Jonah combed his nail-bitten fingers through a tuft at his temple, a self-conscious gesture. "It still catches me off guard sometimes when I look in the mirror," he admitted.

Liam had seen photos of a teenage Jonah—one of the many nights they stayed up texting had involved an exchange of embarrassing high school pictures—so he knew that he had worn his hair long before. Jonah had been *that* version of himself for longer than he had been the buzzcut kid barely scraping by in Chicago. Liam thought it spoke to just how formative the trauma of that time had been, that Jonah still looked for that suffering boy in every passing reflection.

"I like it on you," he said at last.

Jonah hid his smile with another bite of food. "Your roommates are nice," he said. "I've known them for less than a day, but they're already an improvement on your last friends."

Liam couldn't help the sour curl of guilt at any allusion to his former friends. They hadn't spent much time talking about Nathan Scott and the twisted role he played in their relationship to each other, nor the specific way in which he had hurt Jonah. It still sat wrong and undigested in his stomach that Nathan had walked away unscathed. He understood Jonah's reasons for not pressing charges against him: how could he expect him to have any faith in a legal system that had failed him so spectacularly?

Still, Liam thought he might live the rest of his life shouldering the rage that Jonah was too tired to carry around on his own anymore.

"Yeah," Liam agreed. "Too bad the bar was in hell."

"I'm proud of you, you know," Jonah said. "I always knew you would make it here. How does it feel to be actually living the dream?"

Liam's eyes scanned over the view from the fire escape, his own small piece of this place where so many came to find something greater, but they came to rest on the person sitting next to him.

Jonah was a piece of the puzzle that he never accounted for in all his years of dreaming about life in the city, but one that clicked into place like it was always meant to be there. The two of them here, at the start of everything, forging their futures side by side.

"It's even better than I imagined."

# CHAPTER 2
# Jonah

Jonah hoisted himself onto the lip of the truck bed, wincing at the flare of pain in his upper arms. Despite Liam's praise at his feats of athleticism yesterday, Jonah very much felt the aftereffects of the move in his body.

Not that he minded. If there was ever a cause worth aching for, it was Liam Cassidy.

Today's job site was just outside the city limits: a wealthy neighborhood on Long Island, nestled right up against the water. The Great Neck McMansion was under a long-haul renovation his crew had been on for the last few weeks and would likely extend into the fall. Jonah appreciated the job security, and he enjoyed getting to see a side of New York he likely wouldn't have otherwise.

He unwrapped the parchment around his sandwich. His crewmate Beatriz brought lunch from her girlfriend's deli, and she always made sure to grab Jonah something when she went, remembering his quiet delight the first time he ever tried one. He used to think all sandwiches tasted the same until he moved here, but he was quickly corrected on the facts of life.

Tearing off a bite, he swiped at the oil and vinegar that dripped down his chin. He wasn't used to the change in topography on his own hands, the roughness of calluses still an unexpected scrape against his skin. As he chewed, he studied his hands in his lap, turning them over to see the blisters on his palms—some newly formed from the morning of work behind him, some healing in peels of dead skin from the weeks before.

*A working man's hands,* his father's voice surfaced uninvited. The echo was accompanied by a memory of the two of them in the garage, Jonah's tiny, child's fingers dwarfed as he pressed their palms together.

Back then, Jonah had wanted nothing more than to be just like his dad. The strongest man in the world. As he took stock of himself now, he could see the physical payoff of his work this summer. His skin had reclaimed its warm, bronze tone, months of direct sunlight chasing away the last of the gaunt paleness that had stolen his color. There was an obvious change in his musculature, too. Jonah was never going to be *buff,* but he was no longer a collection of skinny limbs and sunken, hollow places.

When he took another bite of his sandwich, he watched the muscles in his forearm move beneath his skin and felt something like pride. This was tangible proof of the effort he had put into his new life. There was a strange, bitter irony in realizing he now so closely reflected the type of man his father always pushed him to be.

*Your son is a regular blue-collar, hands-on construction worker,* he thought. *And a gay one, at that.*

Smiling despite himself, Jonah reached for his phone. It had been a busy morning, leaving him without a chance to check his notifications since he arrived on site. He was pleased to find an unread message from Liam waiting for him now.

That thrill of pleasure stopped short, however, when he opened the text:

**I want to ask you about something.**

Jonah paused mid-chew and set his sandwich on the paper in his lap. The tiny spike of adrenaline, the sudden dampness of his palms, was ridiculous. He knew that, but it did little to temper his body's reaction. He wiped his oily fingers on his work pants and typed a message in return, hoping it came across lighter than he felt.

**Has anyone ever told you that's a terrible way to start a conversation?**

Thankfully, Liam didn't leave him waiting long on his reply.

**HA! Ugh sorry. I'm nervous ok**

**You know that makes it worse, right?**

Liam's 'typing' bubble appeared and disappeared several times before his next reply came through, in a series of disjointed messages.

**SHIT**

**Ok, so this is hard.**

**Because this feels like the kind of conversation to have in person.**

**But now I've already opened the door.**

***Liam…***

**NO SORRY**

**It's not anything about you**

**I mean**

**It is**

**But it's nothing bad**

**I PROMISE**

**Shit. Doing a bad job. Hang on a second.**

Jonah was about to put them both out of their misery and hit the call button, but a knock against the side of the truck startled him out of his spiral. He looked up to find Beatriz gesturing at the spot beside him. Her dark hair was tied back in a single, tight braid, the flannel shirt she had been wearing this morning tied around her waist.

"Mind if I join you?"

Jonah nodded to the open space and forced himself to take another bite. His body desperately needed the fuel, so he couldn't let his anxiety stop him from eating. Bea kept a couple feet of distance between them as she went to work unwrapping her own sandwich.

She was older than Jonah, maybe in her early thirties, and she had immediately taken him under her wing from the very first job. Bea had the uncanny ability to read Jonah's unspoken cues for space. She never touched him with a casual clap to the back or a bump to the shoulder as so many of the crewmen did. Jonah had even seen her covertly step between him and some of the more enthusiastic guys, providing a barrier.

Antonio Ellis, the man with whom Jonah had a complicated past and an unusual present, had promised him that none of his construction pals knew about Jonah's trauma when he hooked him up with this job. Some people, Jonah supposed, just had an innate instinct for empathy. Liam had been the first person to prove that to him.

"How's your boyfriend?" Bea asked around her first mouthful, shooting him a sly grin that Jonah staunchly ignored.

"I never said he was my boyfriend."

Bea snorted. "Sure. I always look at my phone like that when I'm texting my *bros*."

"How do you know that's who I'm texting?"

"Is it?"

Jonah's avoidant silence was all the answer she needed to have a fresh grin splitting her face.

The truth was, Jonah wasn't lying. Not technically. He didn't know if Liam was his... his *anything*, really. They hadn't put a label on it. But Beatriz wasn't wrong, either. With or without the words to describe it, what he and Liam had was more than friendship. If he was honest with himself, it had been for a long time. At least for Jonah.

The day Liam told him about his acceptance to Fordham's art program, a countdown had begun.

Even if they never said it outright, both of them knew that moving to the same city would put them at level ground in a way they had never experienced. There was a silent expectation that it would change their relationship inevitably, though it was hard to predict exactly what that meant. But the truth of it was there all along, waiting for one of them to gather the courage to say it out loud.

Jonah had thought last night might have been that moment.

He and Liam had stayed on the fire escape long past sundown, abandoning their post only long enough to buy a cheap bottle of champagne from the liquor store on the corner. They drank straight from the bottle, passing it back and forth with fingers that brushed with every exchange just because they could. The bubbles had been cold on his tongue, but they went down warm, a loosening agent that had him melting against the brick wall. It was reminiscent of the only other time they drank together, every sip bolstering Jonah's confidence, weakening the fortress he had built around his heart.

Any iteration of Liam within touching distance would have gotten his heart racing, but the details of last night wove the scene into something bordering on a fairytale. The sunset dancing in Liam's red hair, the glow of sweat and happiness bright on his skin, the city he had worked so hard to make his home blanked around them.

Each time their hands brushed, they had lingered just a little bit longer. Jonah was almost sure that Liam felt it too; a slow, gnawing hunger like a third presence, urging them closer.

Jonah had wanted to kiss him.

The longing had grown to a peak after the last strips of pink faded from the sky, leaving them to bask in the pale glow of the streetlamps. It was getting late, but where Jonah should have been exhausted from the long day, his skin had buzzed with undue urgency, as if this one night with Liam was all he had. Perhaps, he realized, it was muscle memory. Clinging to Liam and then losing him when morning came was a cycle that had worn him paper-thin once upon a time.

It didn't need to be like that anymore. They didn't have to hurry.

So when the moment came like a fork in the road, a pregnant pause that waited for a kiss, a declaration, an invitation to stay, Jonah instead let himself be held by the reassurance that Liam would still be there tomorrow. That something as sacred as what they had shouldn't be rushed.

Jonah had been the one to provide the out through the excuse of an early shift the next morning. Liam, of course, had accepted without a trace of disappointment. He'd only thanked Jonah again for his help, then pulled him into an embrace that clung to Jonah the whole way home.

"Speaking of," Bea said. "Loverboy's a painter, right?"

Jonah pointedly ignored the nickname. "He's an artist, yeah."

"He any good?" Beatriz asked, which made Jonah snort a laugh.

"What kind of boyfriend would I be—*your* word, not mine—if I said no?"

Bea narrowed her eyes. "Is that your way of saying he sucks?"

Jonah laughed again, nearly choking on his food.

Early on, Liam had specifically told Jonah that painting wasn't his strong suit, but Jonah had watched him work hard to strengthen his portfolio before he submitted his applications. They'd spent long nights over silent video calls, Jonah immersed in his books while Liam spun a pallet of colors into something beautiful. Even if Liam would never admit it himself, Jonah had no qualms about bragging on his behalf.

"He doesn't *suck*," he said. "He's really good, actually." He knew his tone betrayed a little too much affection, so he barreled on before she could comment. "Why do you ask?"

Bea nodded toward the McMansion. "Sal says the Martins are looking to commission someone to do a mural for the nursery. Asked if I knew anybody. It will probably be under-the-table, but a job is a job."

The fact that her first thought was to ask about Liam, that she'd remembered this offhand detail about someone Jonah cared about at all, was so unexpectedly touching that it took him a moment to form a response.

"Yeah," he said finally. "I'll ask him. Thank you, Bea."

His phone buzzed on the truck bed next to him.

"Don't let me keep you." Bea smirked, pointing down at the message that illuminated his screen.

**Can I call you really quick?**

But it was Jonah who called instead.

It was still a miracle to him: the fact that he could dial Liam's number at any time he wanted and get the instant pleasure of hearing his voice. There was nothing he could do to hide his smile from Beatriz as he hopped off the ledge of the truck and ambled toward the house. He claimed a spot on the wooden patio swing and pressed the phone to his ear.

"Hi," Liam answered sheepishly on the first ring.

"We're switching to carrier pigeon if this is how you're going to text now."

A bright laugh crackled through the phone, and Jonah could already breathe a little easier at the sound.

"I can't promise it would be any better," Liam said. "It would just take even longer to clear up misunderstandings."

"For the record, I'm still waiting to clear *this* one up," Jonah said. "And by the way, I have something to ask you, too."

"Oh? You go first."

"I don't think so," Jonah said. "I'm making *you* wait this time."

"Seems a fair punishment." If a smile could be heard over the phone, Liam's would be radiant. Then he drew in a breath. "Okay. Well. Here goes."

When that was followed by a long pause, Jonah pinched the bridge of his nose. "Liam," he groaned.

"Sorry! Okay, listen. I know it would probably be more... romantic, I guess, to ask in person. And I wanted to ask you last night before you left, but we were both exhausted and, frankly, I may have chickened out a little bit. But the point is—" His voice softened around a swallow. "Would you like to go on a date? With me?"

Jonah didn't mean to go quiet. In hindsight, he understood how that might have been misconstrued into something panic-inducing for Liam, but for a moment he was rendered breathless. At the simplicity of the question. At the purity of it. At the fact that this was his reality, well within reach.

"Like, a real proper date." Liam rushed to fill the silence. "I know we've already, like... I don't mean to imply that I don't consider all of our previous times together *real*—because I do! I just—"

"Yes."

There was a quick, stunned pause before Liam said, "Really?"

A surprised laugh tumbled out of Jonah. "Yes, *really*. Did you actually think I would say no?"

"I don't know! I at least wanted to be open to the possibility of it."

"There was never any possibility of me turning you down." Jonah didn't necessarily mean for the words to surface so easily, so casually, but they were the truth. Liam must have felt that over the phone, because he went momentarily quiet again.

*Soft* was the only word he could assign to the beat of silence that passed between them.

"Okay. Good." Liam recovered, clearing his throat. Then, "Wait. Sorry, what did you want to ask me?"

A smile curled at Jonah's lips. "I guess you'll have to wait until our date to find out."

# CHAPTER 3
# Liam

There was very little practicality in commuting from Manhattan to Queens to pick Jonah up for a date in Brooklyn. Even more so because Liam didn't have a car anymore, so *"picking up"* really just meant *"riding beside him on the same train he would have taken anyway."*

But Liam wasn't going for *practical*.

Jonah Prince was worth far more than a consideration for logistics. This night, this endeavor of pursuing him as something real, was about making Jonah see just how much better he deserved from the people who claimed to love him. He deserved the whole experience: the flowers, the chivalry, and the determination of a man who would do anything to prove himself worthy.

And, if Liam was being generous with himself—which he tried to do with more frequency these days—maybe *he* deserved something like that too.

His short-sleeve shirt was too thin to be *technically* considered sweater material, but it was just thick enough to make him rethink his choices. Sweat trickled down his spine by the time he made it to the front porch of the house in Forest Hills, making the shirt cling damply to his lower back.  He pinched the collar and tugged at it a few times, hoping to generate some airflow as he walked up the brick sidewalk.

The house, along with the rest of the neighborhood, was even nicer than Jonah had described, all  dark red brick and Tudor-style gables and vintage charm. Part of Liam was loath to admit how much he liked it, because it meant paying a compliment to the man who owned it. But Liam was good about keeping those particular opinions to himself.

The bouquet of flowers crinkled under his palm as he switched hands to knock on the door. He switched hands a few more times as he waited, suddenly self-conscious of the impressions his nervous fingers would crush into the wrapping. The longer he waited, the more reasons he conjured to be nervous (as if he were lacking for options). Did Jonah even like flowers? Did he happen to be allergic to the exact type that Liam picked out? Was this too much? Was *Liam* too much?

The door opened, and Liam straightened his back. Jonah stood in the entryway, looking like a dream in all black: a short-sleeved button-up cuffed at the arms paired with ripped denim. Liam thrust the flowers toward him before he could do something stupid like surge forward and kiss him right there on the doorstep.

Jonah's gaze moved from the bouquet to his face, then back again. "You got me flowers?" he said in lieu of a greeting.

It was harder to feel self-conscious about the gesture when he sounded so awed.

"There was a shop just off the train. I couldn't resist."

Jonah took the bouquet, handling it like something fragile, and brought it just under his nose. He closed his eyes for a moment, then looked up at Liam through the petals. "Thank you," he said.

*"No problem"* felt like too casual a response, and *"I would literally die for you"* fell somewhere on the other extreme end of the spectrum, so Liam let a smile do the talking instead.

"I should probably put these in water before we go?" Jonah said, considering the flowers like he didn't know the protocol. He stepped back against the open door and gestured inside. "Want to come in for a minute?"

"Oh." Liam glanced past Jonah, into the wood-paneled hallway behind him. It looked like the inside of a haunted mansion in a scary movie, which only made Liam, begrudgingly, like it more. "Yeah. Sure."

Liam found himself looking in both directions as Jonah led him out of the hallway and into a large kitchen off the main room.

"He's out of town," Jonah said. When Liam's eyes snapped to him, he was met with a knowing smile.

He probably should have been embarrassed at his own transparency, but his posture relaxed at the confirmation that they were on their own. Even if Liam was good about keeping his less-than-complimentary thoughts about Antonio Ellis to himself, Jonah wasn't entirely oblivious to his distrust.

"Wow. A house to yourself, huh?" Liam didn't catch the possible interpretations of that until it already left his mouth, so he scrambled to keep talking. "You were right about it being fancy. Very old school.

Feels like there's a ghost named Clarence living in the walls or something."

Jonah reached into an espresso-dark cabinet to retrieve a glass. "How did you know?" he deadpanned over his shoulder. "I'd introduce you, but he actually can't come in direct contact with sunlight. Maybe another time."

Liam leaned back against the marble countertop. "I think you're thinking of vampires?" He glanced around at the dark, moody furnishings. "Which, honestly, kind of fits the vibe, too."

"Right, my mistake." He could make out the curve of a smile from the side of Jonah's face as he worked, unwrapping the paper from the bouquet. "Clarence is the vampire in the attic. Edwin is the ghost in the walls."

"I'd read that book," Liam said. "Sounds very gay."

"You wouldn't believe the complicated history between these two."

"I can feel it in the air." Liam waved a hand in front of him. "You could cut the sexual tension with a knife."

Jonah brought the glass of water and the bouquet to the counter next to Liam—the closest spot to the window—and meticulously arranged the flowers so there were no uneven gaps. When he was happy with it, he nudged the makeshift vase back from the edge of the counter and turned his attention to Liam.

"No one's ever gotten me flowers before," he quietly admitted.

*I want to give you the world,* Liam thought. *I want to give you back every soft moment that was stolen from you.*

"Well." He clapped his hands together, determined not to choke up before this date could even begin. "Shall we give Clarence and Edwin some privacy?"

■■■■■■■■■■■■■■■■■■■■■■■■■■■■■■■■■■■■■■■■■■■■■■

Brooklyn Bridge Park was Liam's favorite place in the city.

Once, during Liam's senior year of high school, he'd come to the city with his Advanced Art class on a school trip. They'd spent the afternoon at a pop-up exhibit in DUMBO, and after, the class had been allowed to disperse in small groups to explore the neighborhood. In a rare moment of rebellion, after being imposed as a third wheel on a pair of his classmates, Liam had broken off on his own.

He would never forget the moment he'd cleared the last of the renovated warehouses and stepped into the park. Right on the rocky shore of the East River, the Manhattan skyline opened up around him, bracketed by two towering bridges that stretched between the islands. It was the kind of vast beauty that made everything in his mind and body stand still. There was something serendipitous, something *inevitable* about that moment; somewhere in time, pieces shifted into the shape of a promise. A prophecy. The enormity of the city seemed to embrace Liam where he stood, rather than swallowing him up. *One day*, it whispered to him, *you'll be here to stay.*

It had been easy to sell Jonah on the location for their date. "*I'm looking forward to seeing the city through your eyes,*" he'd told Liam, apparently oblivious to the effect of a statement like that dropped in casual conversation.

Liam couldn't help but watch Jonah's expression now as they stepped onto that same grassy knoll, paying him the same reverence he had once paid to the skyline. Jonah's brow lifted, his lips parting just slightly. The perfectly clear sky and the silver, glassy monoliths across the river sparkled in his eyes.

"What do you think?" Liam asked, hanging on every twitch of his reaction. "Amazing, right?"

He was so busy watching Jonah's face that the brush of contact at his hand surprised him. Without hesitation, he spread his fingers and let Jonah push his through, reveling in the terrain of calluses on his palm.

"Yeah," Jonah agreed. "You did good."

Liam wanted to frame this moment behind glass.

"Hungry?" he asked.

Jonah squeezed his hand. "Lead the way."

That morning, Liam had rolled up an old, faded blanket and stuffed it into a tote bag. He spread it out flat now, at the highest part of the hill, enlisting Jonah's help as the breeze off the river tried to fold it over on itself. They kicked off their shoes to use as weights at the four corners and settled down to unpackage their dinner.

They had decided on takeout from the food hall just behind the park, so they could each choose an item from a different spot and split the spoils down the middle. Jonah insisted on paying for both meals, and Liam didn't argue. He could tell how much it meant to him to finally have the means to return the favor of a purchased meal.

And, as Liam wryly pointed out, Jonah was the only one with a job these days.

They pulled their food from the paper bag and spread the feast between them.

"This might be a first as far as food pairings go," Liam said, eyes scanning from the rainbow roll to the carton of chocolate covered strawberries.

"This is a first for me in general," Jonah said, pointing to Liam's chosen dish.

Liam's mouth popped open. "Wait, what? You've never had *sushi*? Like, ever?"

"My family wasn't known for their worldliness." His self-deprecating smile just barely took the edge off the casual mention of his family—a subject he rarely brought up since leaving them behind in the house that nearly suffocated him. Liam didn't let himself linger on it.

"We must rectify this immediately," he said seriously, ripping the paper packaging off a pair of chopsticks and handing them over.

Jonah fumbled gracelessly with them. It was impossibly endearing, watching the clumsy way his fingers struggled to hold them in place. Twice, when he tried to use them to pick up a piece of the salmon roll, one of the sticks clattered to the blanket. Liam, shamelessly eager for any excuse to touch Jonah's hand, offered his assistance.

The sight of their fingers overlayed—pale against bronze, long and thin curled around knobbed and callused—sent his stomach tumbling. He could have gladly sat there all night, touching Jonah's skin under the guise of instruction, but then he got a better idea.

"Open up?" Liam said, picking up a piece of sushi with his own chopsticks. Immediately, his brain fired off with red-faced regret at his own suggestive word choice, but Jonah only raised a brow.

"Are you going to make airplane noises with it, too?"

"If you want," Liam said. Then, in a sing-song voice, *"Here comes the plane."*

Jonah's mouth opened on a laugh, and Liam placed the food gingerly on his tongue. He watched Jonah's reaction, eager for him to like this thing he was sharing with him. When he finally swallowed, he tilted his head.

"Cold fish is a new sensation," he said. "But I see the vision. Going to need another piece to confirm."

Liam smiled.

By the time they reduced their picnic to scraps, the sun had begun its slow retreat toward the horizon, painting watercolor clouds behind the Manhattan skyline. Jonah indulged him when Liam asked to take a photo, stretching out a long arm to capture as much of the view behind them as possible. He stared at it for a few long seconds and realized it was the only photo they'd ever taken together. He made a mental note to change that. Thoroughly.

When the daylight had all but faded, they folded the blanket back into a neat bundle and slipped on their shoes for a walk along the river.

Liam was the one to reach out a hand first that time, holding his breath until Jonah took the offer.

"I believe you were going to tell me something," Liam prodded as they wandered, river water sloshing noisily against the side of the walkway.

Jonah smirked. "I don't know. Do you think I've waited long enough yet?"

"Jonah Michael Prince."

He snorted (a sound that Liam filed away inside his brain to replay later). "Okay. Fine. You know that house in Long Island my crew has been working on? They're looking for a painter, and I gave them your name."

"Oh." Liam blinked. "I mean... physical labor has never been my strong suit, but a job is a job. I can roll up my sleeves and get to work."

Jonah's smile twitched like he was holding back another laugh. "Well, that's good to know. But I think we're talking about two different kinds of painting here."

Liam's steps slowed beneath him, and Jonah followed suit, coming to a stop along the chrome railing that separated them from the water.

"They want someone to paint a mural for their nursery," Jonah explained. "It's not just throwing paint on a wall. It's a commission for your art."

Liam was momentarily speechless. When he did manage to speak, it was only a breathless *"What?"* that made it past his lips.

"It's not a sure thing yet," Jonah went on. "Ultimately it's up to the homeowners, and I didn't want to share any of your work samples without your permission, but they already said they would look at them. I guess the mom is a Fordham alumnus, so she has a soft spot for you already."

"That's like…" Liam shook his head, grasping for words. "Jonah, that is a huge deal. That feels way above my paygrade."

"It's not," Jonah said immediately. "Well, I don't know how much they're paying. Maybe a decent amount? These people are incredibly rich."

"Oh my god—"

"But," Jonah cut in, "I know that your art is worth it. I've seen what you can do, Liam, and I wouldn't lie to you, or set you up for something I thought you would fail at. This is an opportunity to get paid for something you love, and you deserve it."

"Jonah, I…" Liam thought he was going to pitch over the side of the railing and into the water. He thought he was going to leap forward and kiss Jonah until he couldn't breathe. "I don't know what to say."

"Say you'll consider it. Say you'll at least send them some paintings of yours to look at."

And because Liam was weak for Jonah in a way he had never felt in the presence of anyone else, and because Jonah had done this incredibly kind, incredibly thoughtful, incredibly lovely thing for him, he said, "Yeah. Okay." He swallowed, trying to wrap his head around the turn this conversation had taken. "Thank you, Jonah. I don't even know how I could ever repay you for this."

Jonah kicked the toe of his boot against Liam's shoe. "Now you know how I feel."

The train out of Brooklyn Bridge Park was crowded, but they managed to snag a seat after only a couple of stops. Liam was relieved, and not just from the opportunity to rest his feet after a long walk. It didn't escape his notice, the way Jonah held himself in large crowds, and especially in the confined spaces of a shoulder-to-shoulder train.

He was good at playing it off. One thing he had always known about Jonah was how skilled he was at suffering in silence. Particularly if it meant sparing Liam's feelings. Still, Liam clocked the small cues of Jonah's anxiety he had come to learn over time: the way his knuckles went bloodless-white around the silver subway pole, the hard blink of his eyes that held shut just a second too long, his other hand flexing and closing in rhythmic spurts at his side.

Liam tried to be subtle about positioning his body between Jonah and the rest of the commuters, but it wasn't until they were seated that he felt like he could breathe again.

Liam and Jonah fell into a contented quiet, their knees brushing every few seconds as the train rattled north. Anyone else might have resented a commute that took up half the length of a date, but Liam was happy just to be at Jonah's side. It was a rare thing to find someone who could share in comfortable silence no matter the environment. Someone who made the atmosphere with their presence alone.

Jonah had been that person for him from the beginning. For months, they had built castles out of shabby hotel rooms, crafted a kingdom in places where the light should never have reached.

After that, Liam thought, they could make a home anywhere.

Liam was reading an ad along the top of the subway car—some cheeky slogan for a dating app plastered over a photo of two men kissing—when a brush against his arm startled him. Liam turned and found Jonah nodding off, his head lolled to one side. When the train jostled them again, it provided just enough momentum to rock him the rest of the way into Liam's side, his temple coming to rest on his shoulder.

Miraculously, he didn't wake, and Liam didn't dare move a muscle. For several long seconds, he couldn't stop staring down at him—his long eyelashes kissing his cheekbones, the small opening between his lips, the dark hair dangling to his brow.

Liam would never take for granted the privilege of being a safe enough person in Jonah's world that he could let down his iron guard.

They were supposed to part ways midway through the commute, Liam getting off to transfer further uptown while Jonah stayed on all the way to Queens. But Liam watched his first transfer station pass by, telling himself he would get off at the next one further uptown and grant Jonah just a few more minutes of uninterrupted rest.

But when the train approached 57th street—his last chance for a direct transfer—Liam made a decision. He sat and watched the doors open and shut without making a move to rouse the man softly snoring on his shoulder. And as the train hurdled through the tunnel into Queens, he had no regrets about escorting his date the rest of the way home.

Jonah stayed fast asleep all the way to Forest Hills. Liam almost regretted having to wake him when the brakes squealed in approach to his stop.

"Hey." He ducked his head, Jonah's hair tickling his cheek. Careful not to startle him, Liam placed a hand on his arm and gave a squeeze. "Jonah, hey. It's your stop."

A quick jerk of movement was his first sign that he was awake, followed by a muttered apology as he sat up. Jonah blinked, taking in his surroundings through bleary eyes. He looked at Liam, then at the station tracker along the top of the opposite wall, then scrambled to stand as the first light of the Forest Hills station shone through the windows.

"Oh shit. Liam, you missed your stop."

Liam stood after him, holding out a steadying arm as Jonah swayed. "I didn't miss anything," he said, shrugging his tote bag back onto his shoulder. "I just didn't have the heart to wake you."

"I'm sorry. I didn't mean to nod off."

"Don't be sorry," Liam insisted. "You clearly needed the rest."

The train screeched to a stop and the doors slid open. Liam and Jonah trailed out with about fifty percent of the passengers.

"This is so far out of your way." Jonah had to raise his voice over the rumble of the train's departure. "Backtracking is going to add thirty minutes."

"I've got nowhere to be." Liam shrugged, following him up the steps to the mezzanine. "It's not as if I have a *second* hot date after this."

At the top of the staircase was where they had to part ways for real. The subway exit was up ahead, and Liam would have to descend to the other platform to catch the next Manhattan-bound train. A sudden, ridiculous rush of nerves had him swiping his palms against his pants.

"So," Liam began, deeply unsure of how to end a proper date. Was he supposed to thank him? Kiss him in the middle of the subway station? Fucking... *shake his hand?*

"So," Jonah echoed, a smile teasing at the corner of his mouth.

"This was really nice," Liam said. "Do it again sometime, maybe?"

Jonah tilted his head, considering. "Yeah, I could probably be persuaded." And then, before Liam could toil any further over the pros and cons of going in for a goodbye hug, Jonah stepped forward, hesitating only the barest moment before touching Liam's cheek and planting a kiss on the other.

The pure, unexpected sweetness of the gesture left him stunned to stillness. "Text me when you're home safe?" he said when he could find his voice again.

"You're the one hoofing it back uptown at midnight. You've got my ten-minute walk beat."

"Still," Liam insisted, and Jonah conceded with a nod.

"Okay," he said. "You text me, too."

They turned their separate ways, but Liam only made it one step down toward the platform steps when Jonah called out to him.

"Liam, wait."

He turned back, people stepping around him as the ground began to vibrate with the signal of an oncoming train.

Jonah looked almost nervous, fidgeting with his hands in front of him, but his voice was steady when he asked: "Come back with me?"

Something jolted in Liam's chest. "To your house?" he asked, like an idiot.

"If you want."

Of course Liam *wanted*, but the invitation was the last thing he expected. "Are you sure?"

"Yes, I'm sure." There was something like hope in Jonah's eyes when he nodded, not an ounce of uncertainty present.

At the bottom of the stairs, Liam's train was arriving. Without another thought, he stepped back onto the mezzanine and let it leave without him.

▪▪▪▪▪▪▪▪▪▪▪▪▪▪▪▪▪▪▪▪▪▪▪▪▪▪▪▪▪▪▪▪▪▪▪▪▪▪▪▪▪▪▪▪▪▪▪▪▪

It wasn't technically the first time he had seen Jonah's bedroom in the Queens house, but it was a different experience in person. The pixelated view through a phone camera couldn't capture the essence of Jonah that enveloped him as he stepped inside. The innate, familiar scent of him mingled with something lived-in. Cozy, like well-worn wood and clean linens. The space suited him, though there weren't many personal adornments that marked it as distinctly his.

There was a mahogany dresser on the right and a small bed on the left, dressed in maroon fittings that he remembered Jonah had picked out on his first day in the city. The room's singular window was an arch of color above the desk—an abstract mosaic of stained glass that spoke to the age of the home. It was muted now, given the late hour, but he could imagine the way the sunlight dappled the walls during the daytime, passing through to paint Jonah's life in shades of rainbow. The thought made him smile.

Then Liam's eyes fell to the nightstand. He stepped forward, running a fingertip over the smooth, plastic film that covered the first in a stack of library books.

"This is my favorite book," Liam observed. He shifted the top book an inch to the side, revealing the one underneath, and then the one beneath that. Realization crackled to life, a bonfire he could have warmed his hands with forever.

"Jonah, these are all my favorite books. The ones I used to bring with me."

The words floated delicately between them—one of the rare instances they spoke directly about the string of hotel rooms that had woven their lives together last fall.

He looked up at Jonah, unsure of how to hold this inside himself; this new knowledge of how deeply Liam had been seen. Not only had Jonah tucked away these small pieces of Liam's heart, hoarding them for safekeeping, but he had held them close, cracked them open, and looked deeper in a way no one else had ever bothered to do.

Jonah plucked at the hem of his shirt, a nervous tell. "I've been borrowing them on rotation," he admitted. Then, with a softness that betrayed his vulnerability, "They were something familiar in a new place. A little piece of you here."

Liam blinked. Then blinked again, because his vision was starting to go watery, and he was *not* going to lose his cool inside this man's bedroom, on what was technically still their first date. But Jonah couldn't just *say stuff like that* to him and expect him not to die.

Liam thumbed over the stamp of ink on the edges of the pages—*Queens Library*—then slid the book back into place.

"I've missed you." The confession fell out of him before Liam could stop it. Not that he wanted to. Not that he would have. He didn't realize until he'd said it just how desperately he'd needed to get the words out. "I've missed you so much."

Jonah studied him. Then, taking a deliberate step toward Liam, he extended his hand. Liam eyed the stretch of his arm, bronze skin glowing in the lamplight in invitation. His outstretched fingers trembled just enough to be perceptible, and Liam felt the echo in his own limbs, all his nerves resurfacing at once.

"You're here now," Jonah said.

All the distance that had ever tried to separate them—in miles or in circumstance—had finally dwindled to nothing, drawing them closer, leading them here to this room.

Liam took his hand. He let himself be drawn across the final distance. Hands found his waist, warm and solid through his shirt. Jonah curled his fingertips, pressing into Liam's flesh like he was anchoring himself with the contact. When had the faint tremors from the walk home escalated to a vibration that hummed through their bodies? He could feel it in every place they connected: Jonah's hands on his sides,

Liam's fingers sliding over the strong shoulders he had dreamt of touching since that day in the stairwell.

They were so close now. Their record of physical intimacy was a limited one, but Liam preserved each memory like a historian. The night in his bedroom in Naperville, their bodies pressed together in the tight confines of a hospital bed, a private parting kiss before Jonah climbed into his mother's car in the hotel parking lot. A carefully curated museum of Jonah etched into his body.

But of all those instances, Liam had never felt closer to him than he did right now; there were no more barriers left between them.

It was exhilarating. It was terrifying.

Carefully, Liam tipped his head forward, closing the few inches of height to rest his forehead against Jonah's. There was a thrum of something unspoken between them, something that started the moment Jonah called out to him at the train station and asked him to stay and now crested.

Liam refused to make any assumptions where Jonah was concerned. He hadn't agreed to come back with him out of any expectation of what would or wouldn't happen in the privacy of his room, and he was pretty sure Jonah knew that. He *needed* Jonah to know that.

"We don't have to do anything." It was a whisper, but still Liam's voice sounded too loud in the proximity. He dialed back and tried again. "I mean…"

"Liam," Jonah cut in, his voice thick with an inflection Liam had only heard from him once before.

"Yeah?"

"I've missed you, too."

And then he was kissing him. Liam wasn't sure which of them leaned into it first, only that it was inevitable. Once they crossed that line, Liam couldn't remember how he had ever survived a gap in time without this.

It was gentle at first. Liam kissed him back with the care he might have taken to balance a soap bubble on the tip of his finger, but there was a hunger that burned behind it, ignited by the taste of Jonah. A noise that Liam could be embarrassed about later slipped from his throat, and it seemed to shift something in the air. Jonah pulled back, Liam following his lips helplessly for half a second before looking up at him through heavy lids. He wore a flushed, dazed expression, their labored breaths mingling in the sparse space between them. The tips of their noses brushed, every point of contact like a live wire. And then, like a wave breaking on the shore, they crashed forward again, this time without reserve.

Jonah's lips were soft, the lingering taste of chocolate and strawberries layered over the perfect essence of *him*. He molded his palms to the shape of Liam's body, sliding around to his back to pull him in closer. The heat of it shocked a gasp out of Liam, borrowing breath from Jonah's mouth. Their bodies pressed together, chests and stomachs and hips. It was urgent; a sensation that bordered on overwhelming, the way his desire consumed him. Wanting Jonah was a flood. It poured over him, out of him, crashing all his systems. It was almost frightening, losing himself so completely to this feeling. He would have followed Jonah anywhere, done anything he asked of him.

The grip on his waist tightened. Liam complied with the first gentle coax of movement, the slightest nudge backward, his feet stumbling messily under him as Jonah guided him toward the bed. He let himself drop when his legs hit the mattress, but they didn't break contact. Jonah followed him down, expertly slotting a knee on either side of Liam's hips. Liam's hands went to his waist on instinct, pulling him flush as their kiss became something ravenous.

Was this what being high felt like? Jonah's weight, strong and solid, settled in his lap? The drape of his arms around Liam's neck? The smell and taste and feel of him all around him was a drug that dulled the last of his inhibitions.

Liam yielded under the hands that guided him back, falling, falling, falling until he was flat on the mattress. Jonah knelt over him, his face half in shadow but unmistakably wrought with desire. With his palms braced on Liam's chest, Liam could feel every tremor like a current travelling down Jonah's arms, through his fingers, down to the marrow of Liam's own ribcage. He watched Jonah carefully, ready to slow things down at the first sign of apprehension, but he didn't buckle. Instead, he held Liam's eyes and gave the first experimental roll of his hips.

Even through layers of clothes, the movement cut a trail of sparks through Liam's core. His eyes fell shut as his body returned the motion in kind.

*"Jonah."* Liam was a supplicant lost in prayer and dark eyes as he whispered his name.

They had been here only once before—in a different bedroom, in a different state, under much different circumstances. The memory brought with it a burst of clarity, and Liam opened his eyes. He splayed his hands over Jonah's thighs, sliding gently across the denim stretched taut over skin and muscle.

"Is this...?" Liam tried, his throat dry. "This is okay?"

Before, in Liam's old room, things hadn't gone much further than where they were now—hands groping desperately, mouths eager and hips moving. Tonight, they moved with an intensity that made him think it could turn into something more.

"It's okay." Jonah's rough voice spoke shivers into Liam's body. He dipped forward, moving as if to tuck his face into the crook of Liam's neck, but stopped short and met his eyes. "Are you? Okay?"

Liam wasn't sure how he looked right now, but if it was anything like how he felt, he could understand why Jonah felt the need to ask.

"I've never..." Liam pinched his eyes shut, embarrassed. "You know I've never..."

Jonah went still. Liam opened his eyes in time to catch a flash of concern as Jonah began retreating. Liam scrambled to stop him with a hand on his shoulder, pulling some of his grounding weight back onto him.

"No, no, sorry," Liam said quickly. "I didn't mean... That wasn't a *no*." Jonah hesitated for only a second before Liam placed his palms on either side of his face, thumbs brushing over his cheekbones. "It's a yes," he promised.

Jonah nodded. "It's a yes for me, too." Then he ducked his head into the crook of Liam's neck, and time became harder to quantify.

There were a lot of breathless, half-asked questions:
*Should we...?*
*Do you want to...?*
*Can I...?*
A lot of fervent nods and trembling hands and promises—*pleas*—of yes yes *yes.*

The process of unpeeling themselves from their clothes was a lot less graceful than they made it out to be in the movies. Their shirts went easy enough, but there was a lot of awkward shimmying, tangled limbs, and puffs of breathy laughter in taking off their jeans.

The sensation of so much skin-on-skin threatened to swallow Liam whole. It was enough to distract from the self-consciousness of putting himself on display— his pale thighs, the freckled plane of his chest and stomach, the dusting of bronze hair over his body. He couldn't imagine being like this with anyone else.

Having Jonah this way, giving himself so completely in return, was more than he could have imagined before. It was easy to recall the night from the hotel pool almost a year ago, watching beads of water drip down the column of Jonah's neck to gather in shallow pools at his clavicle, and Liam quashing the unbidden desire to follow their trail with his tongue. Even then, even when Liam would have rather died than cross a boundary with him, Jonah had awoken some part of him that Liam didn't know existed.

Jonah's body was different now than it had been in that pool room: sturdier, healthier. But most notably was the smooth expanse of unbruised skin. So rarely had he seen Jonah without the smattering remnants of violence. Liam wanted to put his mouth to every inch of him.

He couldn't help himself. Liam threw his arms around Jonah's neck and clung to him, burying his nose against his shoulder to breathe in the reminder of his safety. The gesture was oddly wholesome in contrast to the heat of the moment, and Jonah went momentarily still. Only for a second. Then, Jonah's body melted into the embrace, tilting his temple against Liam's. He could feel the words there between them, beating to the rhythm of his own erratic heart: *I love you, I love you, I love you.*

Before he could voice it, the hand resting on Liam's side smoothed down his flank, leaving a trail of fire in its wake. Fingertips skimmed the sensitive skin just above Liam's waistband, sending a shiver through his body.

Jonah pulled back to meet his eyes. "Do you want me to?"

God, Liam was dizzy with wanting. His head spun at the idea of Jonah's hand on him.

There was only one thing he wanted more.

"Wait," Liam breathed, unable to keep the desperation from his voice.

In every iteration of this moment he had ever played out in his head, it was Jonah lost to pleasure under Liam's touch. Sweet, perfect, selfless Jonah, who deserved for someone to put him first for once in his life.

"Can I...?" Liam cleared his throat. "I want to touch you. Please."

Jonah drew back. The fleeting hesitation was enough to have Liam swallowing his words, reaching for a retraction or an apology.

"Only if you want," Liam added quickly, his fingers digging lightly into Jonah's bare shoulders. "Anything—*everything*—is only if you want it. It's just... Whenever I've thought about this, I've always pictured being the one to make you feel good. I'd like to try."

He watched Jonah's expression carefully—the twitch of surprise in his brow, the movement of his throat as he swallowed, and finally, the curve of his lips. "You've thought about this a lot, have you?"

If Liam's skin wasn't already an inferno, his embarrassment would have been written all over his face.

But then Jonah nodded, the scratch of his hair against Liam's cheek. "Okay," he whispered.

"Yeah?"

Jonah nodded again, this time rolling onto his back. Liam didn't have time to mourn the loss of his weight, because an arm hooked around his waist and pulled him close. He wasn't quite on top of Jonah, not fully, but enough that he propped himself on one elbow to keep from pinning him down.

They were both breathing heavily, their strained pulls for air the only sound in the room. Carefully, Liam placed an experimental hand on Jonah's stomach, transfixed by the muscles that twitched beneath his touch. He flicked his gaze back to his face. Jonah was watching him with dark eyes.

"You'll tell me if it's too much?" Liam asked.

Jonah nodded a third time. On some level, Liam wished he would vocalize his affirmation, but he knew that this was delicate ground they were treading, and he didn't want to push Jonah for more than he could give. And when Jonah reached up to cradle his face between his palms and pulled Liam back into a kiss, it was easy to let his worries dissolve to dust.

He didn't move his hand right away, allowing them both a beat to acclimate to the new arrangement. Only when fingers slid over his own, guiding his touch lower, did Liam allow himself to breach Jonah's final barrier of clothing.

The feel of him under his hand was intoxicating, but not nearly as much as the noise that spilled from Jonah's mouth as his body arched, his head pushing back into the pillow. Liam navigated his way by Jonah's sounds, by his body's reaction to his touch—a compass in the dark. He was terrified of being bad at this, at being entirely clueless on the subject of making Jonah feel good, but he found that pleasing Jonah came naturally. Liam would have chased any instinct, followed any path, that made Jonah sound like that.

He remembered the colorless tone of Jonah's proposition the night they met—*how do you want to do this?*—and could hardly reconcile the memory of that boy with the one beneath him now. Had anyone ever put him first? Had anyone ever touched him with selfless intent?

This moment of intimacy was so much more than any depiction fed to him through songs and movies and books. For the first time in his life, Liam could understand this burning passion that drove people to make art, to try to put the feeling into a language that could transcend words. And still, Liam knew that it wouldn't have been like this with anyone else. It was because he was here in this room, with this person, that everything made sense. That everything was perfect.

Until it wasn't.

# CHAPTER 4
# Jonah

The first time Jonah had sex, he'd thought he was in love. The night Liam followed him up to his bedroom in the Queens house, he was sure that he was.

It was an insult to draw a parallel between Dominic and Liam, but Jonah couldn't help where his mind took him when his body trembled under a gentle touch. He clung to the stark differences like a man on a ledge, willing them to keep him anchored on the surface: the expanse of freckles like a starry sky, copper hair catching the lamplight, the promise of safety in soft whispers of *Please? Can I? Is this okay?*

Jonah wanted him. The physical attraction was undeniable, but it was secondary to this other, less familiar pull. This otherworldly possession of body and mind made him crave *more*.

He'd known what he wanted the moment he invited Liam back to the house, and the simmering anticipation had followed him all the way home. He'd known what he wanted when he kissed Liam and pushed him toward the bed. By then, there wasn't enough of him left unclouded by desire to allow him to think twice, letting his body move on instinct toward the one person he wanted more than anything in the world.

And it was *everything*. Being with Liam like this set a fire loose in his veins. It was every bit as untethering as it was the first—the *only*—time they did this. That night last December had been one of the best nights of his life.

*Just before it turned into the worst morning,* the reminder whispered from the darkness.

The first time Jonah felt himself begin to slip, it was at the realization of Liam's trembling under his weight.

When he pulled back to catch Liam's eyes, he saw something too much like fear in them. And for a disorienting moment, Jonah saw a teenaged version of himself staring back at him, lying on his back, shaking apart with anxious energy before his first time.

*"God, baby. You're so gorgeous."*

*"Relax, Jonah."*

*"Take this. It will help you loosen up."*

Just a flash of a moment, but the afterimage was burned into his retina. Dominic was a poltergeist in the room with them, a silent hand on Jonah's shoulder, resurrecting the memory of what it was to be the inexperienced one, the one latching desperately onto the guidance of a person he thought he loved. Something cold and uncomfortable shivered through him at the idea that he was filling Dominic's role now with Liam.

*It isn't the same. We are not the same.*

*"It's a yes,"* Liam had assured him, and Jonah let himself believe it. It was easier to do under the influence of Liam's enthusiasm. His pale skin flushed

maroon in patches over his cheeks, his throat, his chest. His head was thrown back as Jonah tasted the crook of his neck, and it was such a headrush to see Liam in this context. The loss of control, the momentary slackening in the taut string of his anxious nature, was an illicit image that Jonah felt honored to be allowed to see. To *provoke*.

Jonah was aware that he was shaking, too, but it was hard to parse out the anxiety from the arousal. The two had been inextricably linked for too long to shrug off, no matter how much he trusted the person in his bed.

It wasn't just Dominic in the room with them. There was no shortage of usurpers come to steal this moment away. Most of them were faceless in memory. A few of them were less so, their features sharper in his mind's eye: the wealthy businessman with the gold wristwatch and tortoiseshell glasses on the nightstand, Shepard's friend with the snake tattoo, Nathan. *Shepard.*

In remembering each of them, it was too easy to remember the version of himself he'd been in their presence: a frightened teenager trying and failing to hide his fear and reluctance from someone who didn't care regardless. Here and now, Liam was willing and eager, and *still* Jonah felt the need to stop and ask if he was okay. To comfort him. He couldn't wrap his mind around how no one had ever wanted to do the same for him.

Jonah was able to keep his head above water until Liam asked to switch things up. The second time he slipped under, it wasn't so easy to recover.

He had given Liam his consent, and he had meant it. Jonah had spent a long time dwelling on the ways his history might get in the way of a relationship with Liam, and he had stubbornly come to the decision that he wouldn't allow it to. Now, face to face with the reality of what that meant in practice, he realized it was the kind of naivety someone like Jonah should have been immune to. When Liam's hand skirted below his waist, the jolt of pleasure was cut with a nameless dread. One that quickly teetered into panic.

Jonah was more sexually experienced than anyone his age should have been, but he didn't know how to do *this*. He didn't know how to have sex with his own enjoyment at the forefront. How to be on the receiving end of something sweet and caring and gentle.

For a while, he managed to keep his reactions locked down. He wasn't ready to cave to his body's warning signs, determined that he could talk himself down before he had to ruin this moment for both of them. It was Liam's first time, after all. Jonah wanted it to be special. He wanted it to be good.

So he kept himself pliant, ignoring the way the separation in his mind was starting to feel a little too similar to his old coping mechanisms—the first appearance in a long time of an old friend he used to call Leo. His whole body was television static. He couldn't feel his hands, but he held tight to his last thread of composure.

Liam was the one to snap it by suddenly stilling his hand. He pulled back from where his face had been buried in Jonah's neck, his expression pinched.

At that moment, Jonah knew he had failed.

"Jonah?" he asked. "Do you not...?"

He had been so deep in his own head that he didn't realize, at first, what happened. Not until Liam's hand pulled away entirely, slipping out from his elastic waistband; Jonah's body had betrayed his efforts of staying in the moment, going limp and unfeeling under Liam's touch.

It had been rarer, in Jonah's experience, that a client's primary interest was in getting him off. Some of his clients liked to do it, though. Henry Becker liked to do it. He would spend endless, agonizing minutes forcing a reaction from Jonah's body, and even longer dragging him over the edge. Calls like that had been among his least favorite. Despite everything that had been taken from him already, there was something that much more demoralizing about his own pleasure being turned into a weapon.

They still weren't done taking from him, he supposed. Even now.

"Are you okay?" Liam asked. "Are you not into this?"

The question, or maybe the tenderness with which he asked it, broke him. Jonah shuddered, eyes squeezing shut against the sudden, urgent burn of tears—the inevitable reaction to the surge of rage and despair that twisted his insides. He turned his head away, mortified and ashamed and so, so desperate not to let Liam see him cry.

Even more horrifying was the realization that he couldn't seem to speak. Words were a blur locked behind his tongue and teeth, suffocating him with their urgency to escape.

"Hey," Liam said, the fear in his voice like a cold bucket of water. "Breathe. It's okay."

Jonah hadn't realized that he *wasn't* breathing. The panic washed over him anew when he gasped for air and found it just out of his reach. A broken, strangled sound cut from his windpipe instead. Both hands reached for his throat.

"Jonah, stop. Please look at me." Liam's voice was distant and muffled in his periphery.

A memory surfaced of the first night they first met: when Jonah had woken in the night trapped inside his body, one foot still in the nightmare he was clawing himself from, only to find a comforting presence at his bedside like a buoy in dark waters.

The memory, and the echo of it playing out in real time, was enough to squeeze the tears from his eyes. Jonah rolled roughly away, onto his side where Liam couldn't watch them fall. The ability to breathe made its slow and grueling return.

"Hey," Liam said from behind him, so worried it hurt. "It's okay. Jonah, it's *okay.*"

*It wasn't okay. There was nothing okay about this.*

"I'm fine," Jonah tried, wincing at the crack in his voice that betrayed the lie.

Liam was quiet for a moment. Then he said, "You really don't have to be."

Jonah clenched his jaw so hard he thought his teeth might shatter like porcelain, filling his mouth with bloody, jagged shards. Because that was too much. Liam's words unleashed a torrent of tears that he had no hope of stopping. He pressed his face into the pillow, then, agitated, rocked upright to swing his legs over the edge of the bed. With his back exposed to Liam, Jonah rested his elbows on his knees and dropped his face into his hands.

Humiliation thrummed through him, an entirely different heat than the one he had chased only minutes ago. He resorted to old bad habits, scraping his nails over his scalp hard enough to hurt. In his present state of mind, it was almost jarring to feel a full head of hair between his fingers instead of an uneven buzz cut.

He was here, in the present, in this house that was safe with a man who would never hurt him, but somehow the past was only ever inches behind him. He felt certain he could never outrun it.

"I'm sorry." Liam's voice was meek and uncertain from behind him, a tone that Jonah hated to hear.

"Don't," Jonah said tightly. "*Don't*. It wasn't... It's not *you*." Of that much he was certain, and he wouldn't allow Liam to go down that rabbit hole.

"Do you want to tell me what it *was*?" Liam tried again after a moment. "Not that there needs to be a reason," he added quickly. "You don't owe me an explanation."

Jonah closed his eyes. He didn't agree, but neither did he think he could bring himself to explain it out loud.

It was the memory of another man in his bed. It was the collective memory of hundreds of other hands on his skin. It was the reminder that Jonah carried the grime of his past across state lines, and how he would never be good enough for someone like Liam. Jonah would never be *normal*.

He was twenty years old. He should be able to go on a date with a boy he liked—one that he *loved*—and then bring him back to his room without a chorus of malevolent spectators circling his bed.

He couldn't say that to Liam. He couldn't say anything. He didn't have the words, so he settled for a sharp jerk of his head.

"Okay," Liam said. "That's alright." Then, "Is there something I can do?"

*You could leave,* a cruel voice itched at Jonah from the darkest corner of his mind. *You could run away now and never look back. Find someone who isn't broken beyond repair and save us both the pain of watching me ruin this thing between us in agonizing slow motion.*

But even the thought of speaking that into existence—the thought of Liam heeding the advice and walking out of his room—opened a chasm of dread in his chest.

"I think," Jonah began, licking the dry lips that still buzzed with the memory of contact. "I just need a minute?"

"Of course. Take all the time you need."

He tried to take that to heart, to convince himself that Liam's patience and understanding wasn't a lie. That it was, in fact, the truest thing Jonah had ever known. He allowed himself a few deep breaths, then nodded, a silent confirmation that he was back inside his own body for the moment.

"Jonah?" Liam began. "Can I touch you?"

Jonah hesitated, distrustful of his own reactions. But this was Liam, and Jonah knew his touch would be safe. He knew that Liam would back down the moment Jonah asked him to. For that reason, he allowed himself to say, "Yes."

A moment later, a palm flattened against his bare back. Jonah took a deep breath, Liam's hand moving with his expanding ribcage, like his touch was an extension of Jonah's own body. Liam dragged his hand slowly up his spine, then back down.

"Just this," Liam whispered, repeating the motion in gentle, steady strokes. "Just like this, nothing more. Is that okay?"

Jonah nodded.

Minutes passed, and the tension began to ebb under Liam's steady ministrations. Jonah's jaw unclenched, the stiffness in his neck receded little by little. Liam must have sensed him relaxing into his touch, because the movements changed a little on his next stroke, his thumb dragging a smooth line of pressure along the inner edge of his shoulder blade.

Jonah sighed his encouragement, and Liam repeated that same pattern a few more times before bringing his other hand to the opposite shoulder. The mattress shifted as Liam settled onto his knees behind him.

"Still good?"

Jonah reached for his voice. "Yeah," he managed. "It's good."

Liam wasn't particularly skilled at the art of massage. His hands were awkward and uncertain, struggling to find the right pressure and hit the right marks, but it was so earnestly Liam, and it was exactly what Jonah needed.

When the last embers of his panic burned out, a residue of shame was left in its wake. His hands no longer shook, but they were damp with cold sweat as he placed them on his thighs.

"I think..." Jonah pulled in a breath, his words careful and steady. "I'm okay now. I can try again."

Liam's hands stilled on his shoulders, then pulled back entirely. The sudden loss of his touch was like stepping off a moving walkway and onto solid ground, a jolt to Jonah's equilibrium that had the world rocking beneath him. The bed shifted again as Liam crawled toward the edge, swinging his legs off so that he was sitting next to Jonah. He didn't touch him, but his gaze was a steady burn against his cheek.

"Jonah, you don't have to do that."

"I *can*. I know how to do this."

He thought he saw Liam flinch in his periphery and only then realized how that sounded. "You can understand how that might not be the most encouraging thing to hear?"

Jonah shook his head. He was messing this up again. "I didn't mean it like that. I meant... I'm really okay now, I just—"

"Nothing has to happen tonight," Liam said. "It's okay."

Jonah grimaced down at the floorboards between his sock feet. "I made you come all the way here for nothing."

"'*For nothing?*'" Liam leaned down to try and catch his eye. "I came here to *be* with you, Jonah. Because I wasn't ready for the night to end. It was never about..."

He waved a hand in the general direction of the bed behind them.

Jonah pinched his eyes shut, shaking his head. "There's usually a certain *expectation*"—he swallowed the word—"when your date invites you back to their house."

"Jonah, I've shared a lot of rooms with you. Most of them with beds. We've never had to take our clothes off for you to hold my interest."

That was exactly why Jonah wanted to now.

"I want this." Jonah's voice was raw when he finally looked up at him. "I don't think it's a secret that I've wanted this with you for a long time, and now that I—*we*—finally have the chance, I..."

"You what?"

*What indeed?*

Jonah swallowed. "I told you, back in Chicago that I didn't know how capable I was of doing something like this. I had hoped that by now things would be different. I thought they might have been. I don't like that I was wrong."

Liam's expression was so genuinely sad that Jonah had to look away again, until Liam called his attention back to him with a soft, "Hey." Jonah looked up. "Do you remember what I said back to you that night?"

Jonah did. Liam had promised that he wouldn't put time constraints on Jonah's recovery, and Jonah had clung to that promise for months with bleeding fingers.

"Did you think there was an expiration date on that?" Liam asked. "There wasn't. And even if there was, I'm sure it would stretch further than *months* after everything you've been through."

"I'm sorry." Jonah didn't know what else to say.

"Don't you dare," Liam told him. "If I can't apologize for this, neither can you."

Exhaustion draped over him like a weighted blanket. His body reeled from the peak and the subsequent crash of adrenaline. He couldn't push back against Liam's claims, and why would he want to? He was offering Jonah an out he couldn't afford not to take.

Liam's hand landed on the mattress between them, palm down on the sheets. Jonah didn't need to think twice before placing his own on top and pushing his fingers through the spaces between Liam's.

"It's okay," Liam told him. "Everything is going to be okay."

Jonah wanted so badly to believe him.

# CHAPTER 5
# Liam

The stained-glass window above Jonah's desk was as beautiful in the first light as Liam had imagined. It was all the more beautiful for the fact that he was allowed to be here to witness it in the quiet intimacy of the sunrise.

Because Jonah had let him stay.

It was the first time Liam had ever woken in a room next to Jonah without the dread of an impending goodbye hanging over them. Despite that revelation, Liam's heart sat heavy in his chest.

As unobtrusively as he could, he propped himself on one elbow to look down at Jonah's sleeping form. Liam had fallen asleep hugging the wall last night, devoted to giving Jonah some personal space. This was after several offers on Liam's part to take the floor or the downstairs sofa or to leave the house entirely. Loathe as he would have been to leave Jonah alone in the aftermath of what happened, he would have done whatever it was he asked.

Jonah hadn't sent him away, though. Liam was especially grateful for that now, getting to marvel openly at the way the rainbow light spilled over his cheekbones, catching the long shadow of his lashes.

"Good morning," he whispered. He longed to reach out and touch him, to kiss him on the forehead where his hair had fallen back to expose an old scar at his hairline. But he kept his hands to himself.

Guilt dripped from Liam's fingertips, stained beneath the nails with the memory of Jonah's suffering and the knowledge that his touch had been the catalyst. Jonah had been triggered, badly, by something they'd done last night, and Liam didn't know how to begin untangling that. He didn't know if Jonah would wake up angry and resentful, or if he would be anxious and avoidant, or if he would want to let the whole thing drop. Liam didn't know which of those options he was most afraid of. Mostly, what he wanted to know was how to avoid ever causing Jonah pain like that again.

He could have stayed there all morning, twisting himself in knots and drinking in the vision of Jonah at rest, but he could only ignore the call of his bladder for so long.

When Jonah didn't stir, he shifted down the bed, inching his way toward the end until his feet touched the hardwood floor. The old house creaked under his weight as Liam tiptoed toward the door and into the hallway.

On the way back from the bathroom, Liam hesitated outside Jonah's bedroom, fingers tapping idly against the wooden banister that ran along the mezzanine of the upstairs hall. He peeked through the crack he'd left in the doorway and found Jonah still fast asleep. Then he glanced over the railing at the staircase and made his decision.

In the kitchen, he smiled at the vase of flowers on the countertop, looking even more beautiful here than they had in the shop, and went in search of coffee grounds. Liam still didn't relish the stuff, but it was his own private secret that he'd been dipping into the stash at his parents' house every once in a while, when the aching absence of Jonah from several states away got to be too much. For Liam, the warm, dark taste of coffee would always be inextricably linked with Friday nights and brown eyes and the feeling of falling in love.

This cup wasn't for him, though. There was no need for soothing reminders when he had the real thing waiting for him upstairs.

The coffee was easy enough to find in the drawer beneath the machine. Liam fumbled through the mechanics and set it to brew while he scavenged for a mug. There was a surprising amount of them for a house with only two residents, and up until recently, only one. Liam found himself rifling through the collection, curious about their owner. There was a dark blue mug with a half-faded college logo that he didn't recognize. Another was impractically spherical, designed as a baseball with a New York Mets logo. There was one toward the back with chipped edges and smears of old paint that spoke of a child's craftsmanship. Sure enough, when Liam nudged the handle with his finger, the mug turned enough to reveal the word *Dad.* He blinked, pulling back.

He was just closing his hand around a nondescript white mug toward the front when movement behind him made him jump. Liam spun around, but the greeting died in his throat when he saw that it wasn't Jonah standing in the entryway.

"Oh." Antonio Ellis sounded almost as shocked as Liam felt to find him in the kitchen. He had a duffle bag slung over one shoulder and dark circles under his eyes like he hadn't had caffeine in days.

Liam pressed his lips together, fingers tightening around ceramic. The last time Liam had seen this man face-to-face was on a darkened hotel rooftop in the dead of winter. Liam had moved to place his body as a barrier between him and Jonah, and he had to fight the instinct to do the same now.

He knew he was being slightly irrational. He didn't particularly care.

"Jonah invited me," he said in lieu of a greeting.

He resented the hint of a smile that formed on Ellis's mouth. "I figured."

Liam bit back the urge to defend himself against the use of his kitchen. This was Jonah's house, too, according to Ellis's repeated insistence. But he didn't seem to mind either way.

"There enough coffee in there for three?" Ellis asked.

Begrudgingly, Liam mumbled, "Should be."

"Thanks. I'll be back down for some in a bit."

*Take your time*, Liam didn't say aloud, though he turned his back on him and hoped he got the message.

The truth was this: Liam didn't know if he had it in him to forgive this man for the part he had played in Jonah's torment, regardless of the role he played now in his redemption. He tried to bite his tongue about his reservations for the most part. He would never stand in the way of Jonah's road to freedom. He trusted Jonah when he said he trusted Antonio Ellis, but he also had to reconcile that with the knowledge of just how many trusted people in Jonah's life had been at the root of his pain.

Ellis hovered in the doorway of the kitchen, fingers tapping against the frame. "For what it's worth, I'm glad you're here," he said unexpectedly. "I think he really missed you."

Liam watched the rest of the coffee sputter to the halfway line in shocked stillness, listening to Ellis's retreat up the stairs.

∎∎∎∎∎∎∎∎∎∎∎∎∎∎∎∎∎∎∎∎∎∎∎∎∎∎∎∎∎∎∎∎∎∎∎∎∎∎∎∎∎∎∎∎∎∎∎

Jonah was awake when he returned to the bedroom, sitting up with his arms loosely hugging his knees. He looked up when Liam entered, though his eyes only lifted as far as the mug in his hands, deftly avoiding his gaze. Liam ignored the twist in his stomach.

"Hey you," he said, perching on the edge of the bed.

"Hi." Jonah's voice was rock salt and gravel first thing in the morning—a sound Liam hadn't gotten to enjoy in far too long.

He held out the coffee, pleased when Jonah's fingers slid over his own to accept it. "Your *roommate* is home," Liam said.

"I heard." Jonah lifted the cup and took a sip. "Thanks for this."

They fell quiet, the distant patter of shower spray starting up down the hall. Jonah sipped his coffee, and Liam tried not to watch him too closely. He was a sight to behold in just his boxer briefs and t-shirt, but there was a clear line of tension in the way he held himself. Like he was bracing for impact.

Liam knew he should say something, that they should talk about last night. Somehow the idea was even more intimidating in the light of day than it had been in the heat of the moment.

He wasn't naive about what he was getting into with Jonah. Even if they had been fine the last and only time they'd skirted the edges of intimacy together, it didn't mean Jonah could shrug off his past like an old coat.

Privately, Liam had been doing research. It felt like too clinical a word for it, but that was what it was at its core: reading whatever he could find on how to be a supportive partner to someone who had the kind of complex trauma that Jonah did. What happened last night wasn't outside the scope of what he should have expected, but that didn't mean he was prepared to handle the reality of it. He recognized that the only way to work through this was to communicate, even if it was hard. *Especially* if it was hard.

But Jonah looked so vulnerable tucked into the corner of his bed, hands tight enough around his mug for his fingernails to whiten. He was waiting for the bomb to drop, and Liam couldn't bring himself to deliver the blow.

Just because they needed to talk about it, didn't mean they needed to talk about it *right now*.

"So," Liam began, hating the way Jonah held his breath as he did. "I seem to recall your rave review of a bagel shop around here?"

Jonah looked up. There was something like gratitude in his expression.

Tentatively, Liam reached forward to wrap his hand around Jonah's bony ankle, just for the tangible anchor of physical touch. "My treat?"

Jonah exhaled. He nodded.

Liam would find a better time to talk about what needed to be said. He would. Just not today.

■ ■ ■ ■ ■ ■ ■ ■ ■ ■ ■ ■ ■ ■ ■ ■ ■ ■ ■ ■ ■ ■ ■ ■ ■ ■ ■ ■ ■ ■ ■ ■ ■ ■ ■ ■ ■ ■ ■ ■ ■ ■ ■ ■ ■ ■ ■ ■

The trouble with attending art school in New York City was that, no matter what skill level you brought to the table, no matter how far you outshot your classmates in whatever advanced placement high school art class you came from, you were most likely to become a small fish in a big pond overnight. For someone like Liam, who already carried an inferiority complex on his back like a boulder, this was a non-ideal headspace to be in. If he had already felt like a small fish in his rural Illinois hometown, what did that make him now? A fucking *tadpole*?

On his first day of classes, Liam spent most of the morning sitting on the floor of his tiny bedroom, surrounded by half the contents of his closet. There was a version of himself that existed in his head; one that was sleek and mysterious and confident and cool. That person wore rare vintage clothes from curated shops and had the permanent contour of a cigarette pack in their back pocket. That person had piercings and dyed tips and painted nails and didn't carry the scars of slurs hurled against him that made him shy away from that kind of self-expression. That person belonged in New York City, belonged with these artists. And *belonging* was all Liam had ever wanted.

It was impossible not to be intimidated by his peers. Going to class felt more like a trip to an art museum. The projects he saw people work over in the student common studio looked like they came with a pretty price tag and the prestige to back it up. Liam tried to remind himself that he was there for a reason—that he had been accepted into this program along with everyone else, on his own artistic merit. His imposter syndrome couldn't argue with the fact that someone along the way in the admissions process had recognized something in him.

But it wasn't just about skill or execution; it was about voice, and the fact that everyone around him seemed to have found theirs while Liam scrambled in the dust. His classmates were the kind of people who had something important to say, and they knew exactly how to say it through their work. He couldn't imagine some of these people—with their vibrant, sharp-edged haircuts and piercings in places Liam didn't know you could pierce and cigarettes in the corner of their mouths that Liam still couldn't quite get the hang of—ever being scared to show someone their art.

"It's all false confidence," Izzy told him. "Everyone is just faking it 'til they make it. Some are just better performers than others."

Which was easy for her to say, because Izzy was exactly the kind of artist he admired so much. For her, art was a form of protest. Her portfolio showed a steady thru line of themes in social justice. The images she created evoked real *feeling* from its viewers—rage, grief, hope.

Liam used to think his art said something. All his life, it had been his way of coping with his own feelings of loneliness and longing. From his current vantage point, those feelings were harder to access. Liam's past felt insignificant in contrast to the last year of his life and all the earth-shattering changes it had seen. There was a defining crack in his timeline, one that formed the night he met Jonah.

Maybe that was the only logical starting place.

He was in his acrylics class, staring down the barrel of a blank canvas, when the image came to him: two parallel beds and two sets of legs dangling in the gap in between, not daring to inch close enough for their feet to touch. Strangers still, but not for long.

It wasn't the first time he'd felt the call to put the memory of that time in his life on paper. One of the first few nights he had spent with Jonah in Chicago, Liam had pulled out his sketchpad while Jonah slept and began putting to paper the details he saw around the room. Small, insignificant things—the wired telephone beside the bed, the lamp and its curved shadow thrown across the wall, the curtains that still held the scent of years-old cigarette smoke. Something he'd never admitted in the time since was that he'd sketched Jonah too. From memory, he outlined the image of him asleep against the headboard, an open book still propped against his chest before Liam had bookmarked it for him and set it aside; a rare moment of peace, preserved in graphite.

The memory of hotel rooms lingered closer to the surface after what happened in Jonah's bedroom the other night. Liam had seen the shadows of the past looming in the dark, and in the days since, Jonah had seldom left his mind.

He didn't realize how much class time had passed until his professor, a stoic French man in his late fifties, began making his final rounds. He came to a stop behind Liam, and Liam rolled back his shoulders, pretending—as Izzy instructed—that all the confidence he'd gained in the last two hours of work wasn't wilting under the scrutiny.

"A hotel room." Professor Olivet's heavy accent and general lack of inflection made it hard to tell if that was an observation, a question, or a judgement. Liam nodded anyway.

There was a rustle of clothing behind him, a shift in posture. Liam was too scared to turn and see his expression, but it was easy enough to picture him with his arms crossed and brows stern as he tore Liam's partial painting to shreds.

But what he said was, "The atmosphere is melancholic. These two, they are in pain?"

His perception made Liam blink. He tried to pull himself out of the painting, to look at it from the perspective of fresh eyes and see which details told the unspoken story. Was it the body language? The way one of the boys in the painting folded in on himself like a protective cage, the other tense and rigid, spine straight with the pressure of performance? Was it the color palette, painting the light inside the room dim and murky like a bad dream?

*They are in pain?*

Liam nodded again.

Another considering pause. "They are lovers?"

A thickness formed in Liam's throat, barely allowing him to get the words out.

"They will be," he said. "They just don't know it yet."

# CHAPTER 6
# Jonah

The house felt alive despite the quiet when Jonah crept down the staircase a little after midnight. The hum of static from a muted television, the kind you felt more than heard, told him he wasn't the only one awake.

It wasn't the first time he had fled his room in the late hours in search of space to breathe, only to find Antonio Ellis already one step ahead of him, sprawled out and awake on the living room sofa. Unlike the times before, though, Jonah didn't retreat at the flicker of blue television light on the wall. He was too restless tonight to confine himself to the walls of his bedroom.

He had never been under any illusion that his previous abandoned trips downstairs had gone unnoticed—the house was too old and creaky for that kind of stealth—but Ellis had been generous enough never to call him on it, always keeping his eyes toward the TV and letting Jonah slink back upstairs without comment. That was probably why he waited this time, not turning his head to acknowledge Jonah's appearance until long after the groaning floorboards had given him away.

Their eyes met, and Jonah held his gaze, almost as if in challenge. To test just how much weight his promise of Jonah's free rein held.

"Hey." Ellis was the first to break the silence. There was something cautious in his voice, as if he were just as aware of how precariously this dynamic of theirs balanced upon a treacherous mountain of history.

"Hey," Jonah echoed. He scuffed his toes against the edge of the area rug, worn and frayed from years of use.

Some rerun of a 90s sitcom played almost silently on the TV, only the occasional murmur of a laugh track audible on the low volume. Ellis gestured to the bowl of food in his lap.

"Are you hungry?" he asked. "There's still some more chili in the fridge."

It was, Jonah decided, an olive branch; one of many he'd extended in the little over three months Jonah had lived under his roof.

One of the first things Ellis did when Jonah arrived in New York at the end of spring was install a new knob on Jonah's bedroom door. He'd let Jonah watch him open it, brand new from the box, and handed him the only two keys when he was finished. He was nearly religious about giving Jonah his space, even if Jonah had seldom left his bedroom for the entire first week. He'd paralyzed by fear that he had made the wrong choice, fear that the city outside these walls would be just as cruel to him as the last. That this shell of a person was all he would ever be, and that no amount of running would let him escape the past that bit at his heels.

Then one evening Ellis had caught him on a trip to the kitchen and asked, the words spilling like he'd been rehearsing them on a loop, if he wanted to go grab a slice of pizza. Jonah hadn't particularly wanted that, but something in him—some desperate part of him that fought tooth and nail toward the idea of life—made him agree.

On the walk to Nona's, a little shop a few streets away with only two tables inside, they passed a library. Jonah set a goal in his mind, a small and achievable task: tomorrow, he would leave the house on his own and sign up for a library card.

From there, the world began to open up around him. He had a full roster of library locations across the five boroughs, nice weather to walk in, and a new reason to get out of bed in the mornings.

Then, of course, Ellis's most significant olive branch (aside from the house Jonah currently resided in, rent free): he had offered him a job.

Jonah was getting better at accepting these small offerings for what they were instead of hunting for the motivation behind them, settling into the knowledge that there was no tally being scored against him in secret.

In the grand scheme of things, midnight chili was easy enough to accept.

Jonah stood with his back against the kitchen counter, arms folded as he waited for his food to reheat. From the adjacent living room, the volume on the television rose a few notches, an exaggerated argument cut with audience laughter spilling in under the hum of the microwave. A lifetime away, he saw himself in another midnight, standing in front of the coffee maker in a hotel he didn't remember the name of. Liam sleepily half-watching the TV behind him, his attentive gaze on Jonah when he didn't think he was looking. The comfort and terror of being seen. The camaraderie of being awake in the dark with someone else.

A shrill beep from the microwave had him blinking away the memory.

He used a paper towel to guard his hands from the heat of the bowl and carried his food into the doorway. He hesitated, deliberating whether to take the chili to his room or read the offer of food as an invitation to stay. Would he be encroaching on Ellis's space? Did Jonah even want to?

Ellis pretended not to notice him hovering until Jonah took a step toward the stairs.

"You can stay," he offered. "If you want some space for yourself, I can head upstairs."

The offer was so absurd he nearly laughed. "It's your house," he said, adjusting the paper towel to shield his thumb from the ceramic.

"Only by the luck of family lineage," Ellis said. "And, in case you need reminding, it's your house, too."

It was not that simple of a truth, even if Ellis truly did see it that way, but Jonah saw no reason to argue right then. Tentatively, he crossed to the far end of the sofa and settled into it.

"You don't have to go," Jonah said after a moment, stilted and stiff. It was strange to give permission that wasn't really his to grant, but Ellis seemed to relax at the reassurance and let it drop.

For several minutes, neither of them spoke. The quiet was surprisingly comfortable, smoothed over by the shared meal and the drone of the television, but it didn't stop the familiar tingle of anxiety that prickled in Jonah's fingertips. He gripped his spoon tightly, the metal edge digging into his skin, and forced himself to breathe normally.

He resented this part of himself that had emerged from the rubble of the last couple of years—the one that reacted poorly to something as innocuous as proximity to another person, even when his brain understood that there was no immediate threat to his safety. Sometimes the feeling would hit before he could make sense of it, all reaction and no logic, and it required him to retrace the steps of his anxiety to find the root. Sometimes there wasn't one, at least not that he could discern.

Sometimes it was this: being alone with a man in the middle of the night, every nerve in his body waiting for the moment a hand would fall heavy on his thigh, fingers would stroke his cheek, would turn his head and—

"I've been seeing someone."

Ellis's words were so unexpected that Jonah had to run them back a few times to make sense of them.

Jonah glanced his way, but Ellis was looking at the TV, his expression carefully blank. A few long seconds passed without elaboration, so Jonah cleared his throat. "Like... a girlfriend?"

Ellis's responding laugh was equally unexpected. He shook his head, some of his tension shaking off with it. "No. I mean a doctor. A therapist."

"Oh." Jonah didn't know what to say to that. Didn't know why Ellis was telling him at all. "Okay," he said. Then, because he was inexplicably curious to know the answer, he asked, "Because you can't sleep?"

"Among other things."

Jonah gave a meaningful look at the clock on the wall. "It doesn't seem to be helping."

His laugh this time was a quiet, self-deprecating thing. "It would probably work faster if I could take her advice on getting a prescription. I was..." He stopped and started again. "I'm an addict. I haven't used in a decade, but that doesn't mean I'm immune to relapse. I don't like to put myself in a position to slip."

This was more information Jonah didn't know what to do with. He thought about the little white pills Shepard used to slip him, back in the beginning, when it was harder for Jonah to quell his body's resistance to the abuse. He could still taste the lingering powder in the back of his throat. He wondered how much Ellis knew about that element of what went on in the house. How much of a threat it posed to his stability.

"It is helping, though," Ellis said. He was looking at Jonah now, his eyes intent. "In ways that are less visible, I think."

All at once, Jonah understood why he had brought this up. His hackles rose.

"I don't want to overstep," Ellis said. "Do you mind if I ask... Have you seen anyone? Since moving home with your mom? Or moving here?"

The idea of seeing a therapist while he lived with his mother was laughable. It was a fundamental truth that had been instilled in him since childhood, that when you face hardships, you turn to prayer. You humble yourself. You search inside for the things you've done wrong in the eyes of God and make yourself clean. To turn to the conceit of man in place of spiritual guidance would be blasphemy.

For the brief time he'd been back in Indiana, Jonah had watched his mother go to her knees every night in prayer as her eldest son wasted away before her eyes. Not once had it occurred to her to get him help from a professional. Not once had Jonah had the strength to ask for it, nor to weather the judgement that asking would bring.

Now that he was here, now that his head stayed above water on most days, that reasoning felt thinner. Old habits died hard, he supposed.

But it was more than that.

Seeking professional help meant embarking on an excavation that Jonah was not ready to undertake. Things he had carefully buried would be dragged to the surface with all the tenderness of a breathing tube ripped from his throat, snagging on flesh, making him choke. He would have to tell someone—a stranger— about where it all started. With his parents. With Dominic. Then, with everyone who came after. He would have to recount the visions he still saw in blood-soaked nightmares. Shepard's face shadowed in the belly of the whale and the weight of his corpse on Jonah's lungs.

No. He didn't want to remember.

*You already remember,* a cold voice whispered at the back of his skull. *You will never forget.*

"No." Jonah winced, surprised to hear the steel in his own voice. "I don't... I haven't. I'm fine." He could feel the burn of a gaze on the side of his face, but he refused to meet it.

"Jonah," Ellis began uneasily, and Jonah was suddenly aware of just how rarely he addressed him by name.

Names had a strange history between them; when they'd met, they'd been Leo and Marcus. He wondered if Ellis, too, had trouble remembering which one he was some days.

"What you've been through would be a lot for anyone to cope with, but especially someone so young. Sometimes I forget just how young you are."

Rage ate through the lining of Jonah's stomach. He bit down on the side of his cheek hard enough to leave an impression. *Young.* Jonah didn't feel *young.* He felt aged beyond his years. Sometimes it felt like his chance to be young was permanently cut short before he could ever truly experience the freedom of it. The only youth he had ever known was a repressed and captive thing.

"No, that's not true," Ellis amended before Jonah could bite back. "I could never forget that. But it's never easy to think about."

Jonah couldn't do this right now. He couldn't have this conversation so close on the heels of his spectacular failure with Liam, the proof of his own brokenness. The idea of going back up to the very bedroom that had hosted that particular humiliation was hardly appealing, but he couldn't sit here and entertain *this* either.

He dropped his feet to the floor fast enough that the spoon rattled in his bowl. "Thanks for the food," he muttered.

"Wait," Ellis said before he could stand. Jonah stopped but kept his eyes averted. "I'm sorry. I didn't mean to chase you out of here. You should stay. I should be getting to bed anyway."

Jonah spotted the lie easily—Ellis didn't look any more ready to fall asleep than Jonah felt himself—but he conceded with a nod, settling back against the couch once more.

He pretended to be invested in the television as Ellis took his dishes to the kitchen and retreated toward the staircase. He paused at the bottom step, the familiar groan of old wood giving him away, even with Jonah's back to him.

"Please, just think about it," Ellis said quietly. "You don't owe me anything. But you owe it to yourself."

# CHAPTER 7
# Liam

Liam was getting paid to make art today. Real, cold-hard cash in exchange for his artistic services.

He had always been a dreamer, but not without a healthy dose of pragmaticism. He understood that pursuing a career in the arts was a risk, and that there was a chance he would never make a cent from his passions. But here he was, less than a month living in New York City and taking on a paid gig.

That he got to do it while spending the day with Jonah only made his first job all the sweeter. While Liam worked on the mural in the nursery, Jonah would be the one-man painting crew for the rest of the house.

"It's cheaper to pay one person than a whole crew," Jonah had told him. "So Sal had no arguments when I asked to have the house to ourselves for a day."

Liam had met with the homeowners on a video call to discuss the details of the mural. The twins were going to be named Robin and Wren, so they wanted an avian theme to match: birds and branches against a backdrop of sky.

They had looked over Liam's portfolio ahead of time, and he thanked his lucky stars that he had really hunkered down on his painting craft this past spring.

They had great things to say overall and pointed out a few of his styles they might have liked to see emulated in the mural. Otherwise, they were happy to see his creative interpretation.

A sunrise, Liam decided. Something that evoked the peaceful feeling of birds chirping at the start of a new day.

Izzy had gone shopping with him for supplies the day before, all of which were being reimbursed by the family as part of his compensation. He'd decided on a palette of soft pastels, with a few darker, earthy tones for the birds.

Having Izzy's expertise at his disposal was a gift. She was only a year above him, but she had gone to an arts high school in New England and had a much firmer grasp on the right types of materials to use for a specific outcome. She never made him feel stupid for not knowing, which probably wasn't a high bar for a healthy friendship, but Liam knew enough to appreciate it anyway.

He boarded the Long Island Railroad at Penn Station before sunrise on a Friday morning and rode into Great Neck. Jonah met him outside the train station in Ellis's borrowed truck. The image of him behind the wheel caught Liam off guard. It hadn't occurred to him until then that this was the first time he'd seen Jonah drive. There was something so stupidly, pleasingly domestic about the idea of riding shotgun with him today.

"Hi," Liam said when he was close enough to be heard through the open window. He hoisted his bag of supplies into the bed of the truck and climbed into the passenger side.

"Morning," Jonah said. His voice still clung to the remnants of sleep in a way that Liam was sure he appreciated a perfectly normal amount.

Classic rock played quietly beneath the rumble of the engine, Jonah having bumped the volume down when he saw Liam coming. The air was crisp and clean this many miles from the city. It was still early enough that the morning clung to its dewy reprieve before another hot day descended on them. Jonah smelled like fresh deodorant and the hot coffee from his thermos. Liam breathed it all in as they rolled onto the main road.

They hadn't had a chance to see each other much since the night of their first date, with Liam's classes starting and Jonah's work schedule picking up in the last stretch of summertime. So Liam couldn't put *too* much blame on himself for failing to broach the subject of what happened that night in Jonah's room. While they'd kept up with their daily thread of text messages, it never felt right to bring up something so delicate without being face-to-face.

Jonah seemed okay, at any rate. He seemed *good* today, light and at-ease in a way Liam wasn't used to seeing on him. Now he wondered if too much time had passed. Maybe dredging the subject up now would do more harm than good.

(He definitely wasn't chickening out. He definitely wasn't avoiding the conversation because he was scared shitless that he would get it wrong).

As they drove farther toward the outskirts of the island, toward the smell of beachy water, the houses they passed grew both in size and splendor. Liam had grown up financially secure in a way he probably took for granted too often, but this was a level of wealth he couldn't touch. He stuck his arm out the window, letting the wind weave through his fingers, and wondered how many nursery murals he would have to paint to afford one of these.

A few minutes into the drive, when Jonah's hand landed not-so-casually on the center console, Liam took him up on the offer.

■■■■■■■■■■■■■■■■■■■■■■■■■■■■■■■■■■■■■■■■■■■■■■■■■■■■■

It was difficult to tell the difference between Liam's usual run-of-the-mill imposter syndrome and a trauma response, but he was starting to lean toward the latter as he stared up at the blank wall in front of him. Stuck in a memory years and miles in the rearview—seventeen years old and humiliated beyond repair—Liam couldn't bring himself to pick up the brush.

He would never forget that morning when he showed up to the park in his hometown, alone at sunrise on his final morning of his city-sponsored mural project. He'd had his earbuds in, something upbeat driving his legs to the tempo. His bucket of paint, or what was left of it by the last day, slipped from his grasp when he first saw *that word* spray-painted over his hard work. The weight had landed on his foot, which had frozen mid step, but he hadn't even registered the pain until later.

Liam was older now. His life was very different than it had been then. It was important to remember that.

There was a certain confidence that strengthened with age, and even more so after Liam had spent the better part of this year proving to himself all the ways he was more capable than he believed. He had worked hard and gotten into an art program in his dream city. He had stood up to the people who had been masquerading as his friends for years too long. He had saved up enough money to land on his feet in New York, landed a paid artistic gig in the first month, and nurtured a relationship that was real and meaningful and good.

He wasn't that lonely kid anymore. There was no one here waiting in the wings to hurl something cruel in his direction at the first show of weakness. There was only him and Jonah and this peaceful morning on the Long Island shoreline, in an empty house that was theirs for the day.

Liam breathed in the ocean air that breezed through the open window, listening to the comforting sound of movement from a few rooms away, the muffled chatter of an audiobook playing aloud. He picked up his phone, already attached to the speaker he'd packed. Careful to keep the volume low enough that he wouldn't disturb Jonah's book, he queued up the playlist he had put together for the occasion the night before. Title: *The Baby Birds.*

He picked up the brush.

# CHAPTER 8
# Jonah

The reprieve of the September morning chill didn't last long. As Jonah worked, the sunlight and the breeze off the water brought with it a salt-sticky heat. By the time his stomach growled in demand for lunch, his shirt clung to skin with sweat. The repeated stretch and pull of a paint roller across a house this size, with its high ceilings and long corridors, was hard work, but it left a satisfying burn in his arms and back.

He had managed to finish most of the upstairs rooms. The only one left to tackle was the nursery. It had taken some restraint on his part to steer clear of Liam's space and give him solitude to work, but bringing him lunch seemed like as good an excuse as any to take a peek.

Jonah grabbed the cooler he had packed this morning and headed toward the sound of music, smiling as he drew closer. When he reached the doorway of the nursery, the sight before him stunned him in place.

He wasn't sure which was more breathtaking—the half-finished depiction of a sunrise on the wall, or the sight of Liam so completely immersed in his element. Both. Either. Jonah was frozen in place, mesmerized.

Liam moved like a dancer when he painted. Like he was born with something in his body that drew him to this work inevitably. His movements fell in sync with the music, a Beatles song Jonah recognized from the radio stations Ellis liked to play in his truck.

And the singing. Liam was *singing*.

The sound was a revelation. Jonah wondered if Liam even realized he was doing it or if it was a byproduct of being so enthralled in his work that he forfeited any self-consciousness.

He could have watched him forever, but the scuff of Jonah's boot betrayed his arrival. Liam yelped and spun to face him, nearly kicking over a tray of mixed paint at his feet.

Jonah was already raising his hands in apology. "Sorry," he said, though he couldn't keep the smile off his face. "I didn't mean to startle you."

"*F-minus* on execution." Liam clutched his chest with the hand that wasn't holding a paintbrush. "How long have you been standing there?"

It took Jonah a moment to find words, because Liam's face was streaked with stray swipes of paint, dappling the space between his freckles with pink, and Jonah suddenly, desperately wanted nothing more than to see that color smear beneath the pads of his thumbs.

"Only a minute," Jonah said.

Liam's face was already red from the heat, which robbed Jonah of an opportunity to see him flush. "Okay, weirdo." He played it off smoothly, folding into a mix of a curtsy and a bow. "Enjoy the performance?"

"Very much." Jonah's reply came out helplessly earnest, so he redirected their attention to the mural. "Liam, this is..." Every compliment fell short on his tongue. "You're so good at this."

Liam's nervous tells were charmingly predictable; the dropped gaze, the way he busied his hand with squeezing the excess paint from his brush. "It's not really anything yet. Just color and outline."

Jonah stepped further into the room, coming to a stop beside him to get a better look at the wall. "It's weird to think that you're painting this for people who haven't even been born," he said. "Like, these babies will grow up and probably never meet you, but they'll spend the first years of their life against the backdrop of something you created."

Liam's eyes went wide, his cheeks rounding with a puff of air that he let out in a long whistle. "Wow. Okay. No pressure or anything."

Jonah laughed and shifted closer, letting his shoulder bump against Liam's. "You're doing great," he promised. "It's going to be perfect. It already is."

Liam bumped him back, his knuckles brushing against Jonah's. "Well, thanks."

The moment went soft between them, in the way it tended to do with Liam. Jonah drew in a breath and cleared his throat, stepping back. He shook the cooler in his hand.

"Lunch break?"

"You made lunch for us?"

"It's nothing too exciting." Jonah rubbed the back of his neck. It was his turn to be self-conscious.

An unexpected skill Jonah had picked up since moving to New York was cooking. Ellis had made it clear on his first day in the house that Jonah had free reign over the kitchen and everything in it. On days he wasn't on a job or holed up in the library or at the park, he spent a lot of time hovering over a stovetop, trying his hand at new dishes.

He'd made a routine of it: checking out a cookbook, then swinging by the grocery store on the way back to the house to pick up what he needed. He always ended up with more than he could eat, leaving a fridge full of leftovers for him and Ellis to share. Ellis had offered to chip in some cash for these expeditions, since he was benefiting from it, but Jonah didn't allow it. Ellis was covering enough of his expenses as it was.

Having money in his pocket to buy fresh ingredients was a privilege Jonah would never be able to take for granted. The whole cooking endeavor had initially been born out of a mind for practicality. He had wanted to spend his newfound income wisely, and learning to prepare his own food was a survival instinct that would help him build the independence he so craved. He liked it more than he thought he would, the act of creating something whole out of a bunch of separate pieces and knowing it came from his own hands. Perhaps, he thought, that was what drew Liam to the art he made.

"Of course it's exciting," Liam said. "It's the first time I get to try your cooking."

"*No pressure,*" Jonah echoed.

They ate on the terrace on the upper level, accessible only through the sliding glass door of the primary bedroom.

The back of the house faced the ocean. It was hard to wrap his head around the idea that this was the view from someone's house. Although the people who resided here would never have quite as good a view as Jonah did now, of a paint-speckled Liam Cassidy smiling in the sunlight, copper curls tossed by the ocean breeze. Jonah wanted a mural of that image painted across every wall inside his mind.

Liam was far more enthusiastic about a lunch that came out of a handheld cooler than anyone had a right to be, but Jonah couldn't deny the satisfaction he felt watching him hum around the first bite, eyes closing in genuine delight. The food was simple enough, because Jonah had been limited to things that could be eaten cold after sitting for a few hours—a sandwich on homemade ciabatta and spicy cucumber salad. Despite Liam's compliments, Jonah insisted he could do better with access to a stovetop.

"I guess you'll just have to cook me a big, fancy dinner next time," Liam said, oblivious to the way Jonah's heart thumped to the beat of that promise.

*Next time. Next time. Next time.*

They hadn't talked about what happened—or what *didn't* happen—that night in his bedroom. Not even the morning after, when Liam had been all soft smiles and careful touches. Jonah suspected Liam was waiting on him to initiate the conversation. And Jonah knew he should. But Liam, as always, sorely overestimated Jonah's bravery.

But now there was a *next time*, spoken into existence like a tiny miracle, and Jonah could breathe a little easier knowing he hadn't ruined everything.

They didn't take too much time to eat, quick to feed the hunger from a long morning of work. Jonah wasn't eager to abandon such a perfect moment, but it was ample consolation that the tradeoff was getting to watch Liam work after the break. So he took a moment to commit the image of Liam against the backdrop of the beach to memory, then they packed up and headed inside.

∎∎∎∎∎∎∎∎∎∎∎∎∎∎∎∎∎∎∎∎∎∎∎∎∎∎∎∎∎∎∎∎∎∎∎∎∎∎∎∎∎∎∎∎∎∎∎∎

Jonah thanked himself for saving the nursery for last.

His body was tired, but sharing space with Liam for the afternoon bolstered his spirits more than any amount of caffeine and a night of sleep could have hoped to.

Liam brought the music back, the volume notched slightly down to allow for conversation. He seemed more reserved about singing out loud with an audience, much to Jonah's disappointment, but his inhibitions seemed to lower the longer they worked together.

By the time Jonah had finished the first coat of lavender on the three remaining walls, the tuneless murmurs under Liam's breath had graduated to resounding belts, occasionally with the use of a wet paintbrush as a microphone. Jonah found it impossible to resist when that paintbrush was extended to him in invitation, the light in Liam's eyes infectious. Jonah leaned in, inches away from smear of canary-yellow paint across his chin, and sang the line he had been prompted. His voice crackled and dipped, a muscle weak from disuse—when was the last time Jonah *sang?*—but naked delight poured over Liam's face as if a chorus of angels had opened the sky.

The lavender was such a light pigment that it needed three coats, but Jonah still finished his portion of the work before Liam. With Liam's permission to openly spectate, Jonah balled up his flannel and stuffed it under his head, lying back on the tarp-covered floor. He laced his fingers behind his neck like he was soaking in the rays from Liam's painted sunrise and watched from between tented knees. Liam tossed him a wry grin over his shoulder, another snapshot Jonah stored away for safekeeping and got back to work.

Liam kept the music low, but neither of them felt the need to carry a conversation. It was clear Liam was fully engaged in the final stage of the painting, and Jonah didn't want to distract from that. He was plenty content to be a fly on the wall, an indulgent witness.

Liam's competency, the rare, earned confidence in his movements, stoked an unexpected reaction in Jonah. The stirring of desire, bordering on a devotion reserved for worship, took him by surprise. But in the safety of Liam's distraction, he let his eyes wander.

Appreciating Liam's aesthetic appeal was nothing new, but allowing himself to consider a physical relationship as something attainable gave it new life. He watched, enamored, as wiry muscles flexed and shifted under pale, freckled skin. When Liam reached up to stroke a silver lining onto the highest cloud, his shirt lifted to reveal a dimpled lower back. It was suddenly impossible not to remember how that part of him felt under Jonah's palm. How it felt to slip his hand lower.

Jonah let out a long, slow breath through his nose. *Painting*, he thought. *Focus on the painting.*

It was less than an hour later when Liam lowered his hands to his sides, took a step back, and stared up at the wall for a long, silent stretch. Jonah watched, eyes torn between the art and the artist, and waited for the declaration. Finally, Liam tossed his brush into a mostly empty tray and turned back to Jonah, one arm gesturing widely.

"Ta-da," he sang.

Jonah pushed himself up, leaning back on his hands. There was never any doubt in his mind that this mural would be beautiful, but what Liam delivered was even better than he imagined. Spindly branches blooming with yellow and white flowers stretched up and out from the bottom corner of the room. In the middle of the largest branch, two small birds sat side by side, facing away from the viewer, their feathers painted in a depiction of iridescence in the false light.

Liam's raw talent was evident, but even more than that, his dedication to the vision was woven into every brushstroke. It was undeniable from even a glance Liam cared about this piece—about what it meant to him as a new artist making his way in the world, and what it meant for the newborn babies who would sleep beneath the glow of his pastel sky.

"I..." Jonah shook his head. "I don't even know what to say."

Liam ran a hand through his sweaty hair. "If you're looking for suggestions, might I recommend, '*Liam, your artistic genius is boundless and incomparable.*'"

A smile spread slowly over Jonah's face. "'Liam,'" he echoed obligingly, "'your artistic genius is boundless and incomparable.'"

"Wow, thank you. That is so kind of you to say." Liam sank down next to him, twisting his torso in both directions in a ripple of pops and cracks.

"They're going to love it." Jonah nudged a water bottle in his direction.

He'd been so focused in those last couple of hours that he'd hardly paused for a sip. Now, he drank like a man in a desert, head tilted back and stray rivulets trickling down his chin, over the smooth column of his throat. Jonah followed the droplets down to the damp neckline of his shirt and swallowed.

"Will you take a picture?" Liam pulled his phone out of his pocket and held it out to Jonah. "Gotta commemorate the moment or whatever."

Jonah gladly took the phone and shuffled back toward the doorway to get the full mural in the frame. Liam scooted the other way, closer to his painted wall. He had his knees bent and loosely spread, both elbows resting on them to throw up twin peace signs. His smile was big enough that his eyes were nearly shut. Jonah took the photo, then several more. Just to be sure.

He made sure to send them all to himself as he stood. Crossing to Liam, he traded the phone back in exchange for an outstretched hand, pulling Liam to his feet. Their hands lingered longer than strictly necessary, so Jonah used it to his advantage, maintaining his hold to tug Liam forward.

"Come on," he said. "It's not every day we get to watch the sunset from a private beach house."

They returned to the terrace off the main bedroom where they'd eaten lunch. Jonah filled his lungs with a gust of sea breeze, held it, then let it out.

"It feels like you can breathe easier out here," he said. "Like the air is lighter."

"Definitely cleaner than that good ol' New York City smog," Liam agreed. "What do you think these people do for work to afford a place like this?" He leaned against the opulent granite railing that separated them from the drop overlooking the beach.

Jonah sidled up beside him, close enough that their arms were in constant contact. He squinted at the horizon. "Definitely in the mafia, right?"

Liam sighed, dramatic and wistful. "Something to aspire to, I suppose." He turned toward Jonah, nudging the toe of his yellow high-tops, now speckled with paint, against Jonah's work boot. "Thank you, again," he said. "For landing me this opportunity. I can't tell you what it means to me."

"I already told you. You earned it yourself."

Liam didn't push back. Instead, he wet his lips, fingers trailing along the balcony rail until they brushed Jonah's elbow. "Can I kiss you?"

Jonah nodded. He wondered if it showed on his face, what it meant to him—the asking. The waiting for consent. The gentleness with which he treated him.

The kiss didn't stay gentle for long, though, and Jonah didn't want it to. He lit up when Liam made a high, desperate sound against his mouth, his hands sliding into Jonah's hair. His fixation with the new length made Jonah want to keep growing it out, letting it run wild in a way he never had, if only it would keep Liam clinging to him like this.

*Next time*, the words echoed again in Jonah's memory. Liam kissed him like there was a future ahead of them, one where their two paths twined seamlessly together. The thought opened up around him like a brilliant light. It opened beneath him like a bottomless pit. He didn't understand how both of those things could be true at once.

Liam pulled back, keeping his fingers light at the nape of Jonah's neck. "What's wrong?"

Jonah shook his head. "Nothing." It should have been nothing. This was the most perfect moment, the most perfect day. Jonah's anxious melancholy had no place here, but it was too late; it'd made its home anyway. "Nothing," he repeated. "Just... earlier. You said you wanted me to cook you dinner next time."

Liam frowned, beginning a careful retreat. "I mean, you don't have to—"

"No, that's not..." Jonah closed his eyes, shaking his head again. He caught Liam's hand as it pulled away, twisting their fingers together. "You said *next time*."

The crease between Liam's brows deepened, which made sense, because Jonah *wasn't* making any sense. His thoughts were getting tangled in his throat like they always did, coming out wrong, out of order.

"You said it so easily," Jonah clarified. "Like it wasn't.... It was just a given. That there would be a next time."

"I'm sorry." Liam's voice was suddenly unsteady. Uncertain. "I didn't mean to assume."

Jonah couldn't watch him suffer a moment longer. "I didn't know if you'd still want this." The truth burst out of him. "Want *me*." When he dared to look up again, clarity had dawned in Liam's eyes.

"Jonah," he whispered.

"I wouldn't blame you," Jonah added quickly. "I know it's not reasonable to expect... I mean you deserve—"

"Jonah. This is about what happened in your room?" He waited for Jonah's nod. "Have you really been worried this whole time that I was thinking this way?"

Jonah eyed him, heart in his throat. "Have you really *not*?"

"No. I haven't," Liam said. "I've been thinking a lot about that night, but not in the way you're worried about." He looked down at their intertwined hands, dangling between them. "The opposite, really. The conversation went a little differently in my head, but I was hoping to talk to you today about this." He squeezed his hand. "About *us*."

All at once, the steady thrum of a promised *next time* was replaced with the cadence of that one syllable.

"*Us*," Jonah echoed, desperate to taste the word for himself.

"What we have has always been real to me," Liam said. "But I want to be able to define it. I want to *call it* something real, too."

It was everything Jonah wanted. It was everything he feared. These two truths stood in tandem, hand in hand, each one nonexistent without the other. He was being offered the love of Liam Cassidy, and the risk of losing it. Jonah had never been taught how to hold something precious like this; it felt slippery in his fingers. In his limited history, love was a fleeting thing, never his to hold for long, always caught on a condition.

Liam had already spent the better part of a year teaching him how to swallow love in smaller doses, and even then it had been beyond the scope of his understanding. He didn't know if his body could hold this much at once.

"You want to be my boyfriend?"

Liam smiled, wry and nervous. "We can talk about labels. But I want a relationship with you, yes. A romantic one. If that's what you want, too."

*Want* wasn't a big enough word for it. Words were rarely big enough when it came to how he felt about Liam.

"I want to be fair to you," Jonah said. "You've never been in a relationship like this. You deserve..." *Better. More.* "Liam, what happened the other night..."

"If this is about sex," Liam said, uncharacteristically blunt, "and whether or not you think that's on the table right now, or ever... Jonah, that's not a big deal."

White static filled all the spaces inside Jonah's brain where a response might have formed. He pushed the words apart and back together again, trying to make sense of them.

"Maybe that didn't come out right," Liam said. "I... No, sorry. Having sex with you would be a *very big deal* to me. That's not what I'm trying to... I'm not trying to diminish the weight that would hold. I'm just trying to say that sex, in general, has never been that important to me."

It was so completely the opposite of everything Jonah had come to learn about the rules of attraction. Men had taught him, over and over, that his body was a non-negotiable in the bargain of their interest. Even the ones who were nice to him. Even the ones he thought might have cared on some level. Even Dominic. That was just the way the world worked. For some, what he could do with his body was the *only thing* that mattered.

It shouldn't have surprised him that Liam was different from the others, even in this. He wanted to understand. Jonah took half a step back without releasing Liam's hand; he didn't want to put distance between them so much as he wanted to be able to read Liam's face more clearly. "Are you not interested in any of it?" Jonah asked. "What we've done already, was that...? I would never want to push you to do something you don't like."

The idea twisted in his stomach like barbed wire. Suddenly Jonah found himself less concerned with what they *hadn't* done and more worried about what they *had*. He mentally combed through every second from his bedroom, from Liam's old bedroom all those months ago, trying to remember if there had been any signs he overlooked, any hesitation he had misread. After all the care Liam had shown him, if Jonah had been the one to inadvertently cross a boundary—

"No! God, sorry. I'm saying this all wrong. I've never really... tried to put this into words before." Liam took a breath. "Let me make something very clear: I've loved every second of what we've done together. And I'm..." He rubbed the back of his neck, pink rising beneath his skin. "I'm very open to doing more. With you. If you want. But *only* if you want. I'm just trying to say it's not a dealbreaker, okay? Not for me."

At the soft tug of his hand, Jonah let himself be pulled back into Liam's space, nodding his assent when Liam raised his arms to wrap around Jonah's shoulders. Their foreheads touched, breaking away only quick enough for Liam to place a chaste kiss on the tip of his nose.

"This could be enough for me," Liam said, placing his palm over Jonah's heart. "*You* are enough for me, just as you are."

Jonah let the words wash over him again and again. He let them run like river water over the jagged stone of his heart, hoping one day it would be smooth to the touch. Looking in Liam's eyes, this close to their brilliant green, Jonah had no choice but to believe him.

"Boyfriends, huh?" Jonah said.

There was a fleck of half-dried paint on the peak of Liam's cheekbone. Testing these newfound grounds of their relationship, Jonah pressed his thumb to the blemish and dragged it under his eye. He laughed when all it did was spread the streak of lavender further across his skin.

"I like the sound of that," Liam said. Jonah didn't know if he meant the sound of *boyfriends* or the sound of Jonah's laugh, but it didn't matter, because then they were kissing against the backdrop of their own private sunset, and nothing in the world mattered but that.

Jonah snaked his arm around Liam's waist and pulled him close, no tolerance for even an inch of space between their bodies. Liam acquiesced like putty in his hands, melting into him.

"Can I just say?" Liam broke away after a minute, breathless and close. "Now that we've made things official? This whole construction worker thing"—his hands slid down from Jonah's shoulders to his arms, where the hems of his sleeves pulled taut against newly defined muscle—"is *really* working for me."

It was so unexpectedly brazen; a new flavor from someone usually so shy and sweet. The laugh that it pulled from Jonah was pure elation. He felt high off the rush. Chasing that feeling, Jonah spun them around, keeping Liam carefully away from the balcony's ledge, and bent down to hook his hands under Liam's thighs. Liam let out a squeal, all surprise and delight, as he was lifted off the ground.

"Is that so?" Jonah asked. His pulse beat against his sweat-sticky throat, so much wild joy in his body that he didn't know what to do with it. "I hadn't noticed."

Liam's fingers dug into his shoulders, scrabbling for purchase as he locked his ankles behind Jonah's back. He was giggling—there was no other word for the heady sound bubbling out of him, like fresh-popped champagne spilling over Jonah's own mouth.

It was a clumsy stumble back through the open sliding door, Jonah's foot nearly catching on the lip of the frame. He clutched hard at Liam's thighs, refusing to break the stride of their kiss as he spun them again, pressing Liam's back to the wall opposite the mural.

The lavender paint was still damp, staining into their clothes on contact, but Jonah didn't care. Not when those long legs were wrapped around his waist, hands in his hair, Liam's weight like an anchor keeping him tethered to earth.

"For the record," Jonah whispered. "I do. Want more with you."

"Whatever you're willing to give," Liam said. "That's what I want."

It didn't feel like *giving* with Liam, though. It didn't feel like he was ever losing anything, trading anything away. The transaction of it was a feeling Jonah was all too familiar with, so he could easily identify the absence of it now.

He lowered his grip on Liam, holding tight until his feet were on the floor. Liam kept his hands on Jonah's shoulders, keeping him close.

"I think," Liam said quietly, "this paint is still wet."

Jonah tipped his head forward to touch Liam's shoulder. "Oops," he said, not at all sorry.

With trembling fingers, he traced the strap of Liam's overalls, playing with the metal buckle at his chest. He pulled back to catch Liam's eyes, watching his pupils liquify with understanding.

"*Oh,*" Liam breathed.

"Stop me if you don't want this," Jonah said.

It seemed impossible, the little thrill of excitement down his spine as he sank to his knees, that an act Jonah had performed more times than he cared to remember could feel brand new in this context. With this person. His fingers trembled with anticipation instead of fear as he tugged down Liam's straps, letting the denim settle below his hips.

Liam was right. They would have to repaint this section of the wall before they left tonight, smoothing over the scuff marks left by their tryst, but Jonah didn't regret it for a moment. Not when he thought about the prints of their hands, the fibers of their clothes, the beautiful messiness of this moment forever sealed into the walls of this house in Long Island. The landmark where they became something they could call by name.

# CHAPTER 9
# Liam

"They didn't have any pre-decorated cakes at the store," Tucker was telling him, "so we took it upon ourselves."

That much went without saying, really. Liam was pretty sure any bakery employee would be fired for sending a product like this out the door. But Izzy and Tucker wore matching grins as they stood beside their pièce de résistance: a small, round cake with the words *HAPPY BIRTH* scrawled in messy pink icing, each successive letter growing smaller with the *oh-shit* realization that they were running out of room.

It was, decidedly, the best birthday cake of Liam's life.

"That sure is something," Liam said, though he couldn't keep the smile off his face. It was incongruously sentimental, the soft, warm thrum of *friendship* he felt at the gesture. Still, he tried to play it cool, turning to Izzy with a raised brow. "I thought you were supposed to be an artist."

"I'll give you one guess who was on icing duty." She cut her eyes to Tucker, who raised a hand.

"It was me. I was on icing duty."

"I thought that might be the case," Liam said. Then, swallowing, he tried not to let his voice sound too earnest when he said, "Thank you. Both of you. It's perfect."

"Nailed it," Tucker whispered, slipping Izzy a low-five.

The apartment was strung with fairy lights and gaudy, mix-matched tinsel they had found in a plastic bin at the back of a thrift store, which the cashier had pinched between her fingers and marked the price as *"I don't know, fifty cents?"* The lights were low, because the lights were always low, because their apartment didn't come with overhead lighting. But Izzy had found one of those color-changing bulbs and swapped it into the standing lamp, which washed the corner of the room in a gradient rainbow show. Liam's Bluetooth speaker on the kitchen counter blasted an appropriately chosen song about being twenty-two from his birthday playlist.

The best gift of all was the *on my way* text that glowed with promise in his back pocket.

It was hard not to think of where he had been a year ago to the day, before the night had taken a hard left turn and sent Jonah Prince barreling into his life to stay.

Tonight, all it had taken was a single word from Liam that he wasn't a fan of crowded bars, and his roommates—his *friends*—had altered their plans to a night in. That they had wanted to celebrate his birthday at all was big enough, but to take into account what Liam needed, to put his wants at the center of attention, showed just how far he had come in terms of friendship in a year's time.

Ben had sent him a happy birthday text that morning, evoking a whole range of emotions Liam wasn't ready to address. He had just stared at it for a while. It was the first he had heard from him since he moved. Frankly, he was sort of surprised Ben remembered his birthday at all. Maybe a memory had popped up on social media. Maybe it was a photo he had taken at the bar last year, or maybe it was the photo Ben had taken the year prior, when Liam had worked a shift at the diner on his birthday and spent the night waiting on Ben and Nathan and their real friends.

His whole body revolted at the unwelcome reminder of Nathan's existence. Sometimes the injustice of how things had been left was an unbearable weight on Liam's chest. Nathan had been allowed to walk free as the bruises he'd left on Jonah took weeks to fade, and even longer for the wounds that didn't show on the surface. Liam hoped, at least, that the scar Jonah had left on Nathan in the end never faded. That he always had to live with a visible reminder of what he'd done.

"No frowning on your birthday," Izzy said, pushing a drink into his hand.

Liam accepted it gratefully, tapping the lip of his cup against hers.

By the time Jonah arrived, the apartment was swollen with bodies. Classmates, friends of friends, and Tucker's various friends-with-benefits sprawled in groups over rugs and couches and the unwieldy bar stools Tucker had found on the sidewalk on trash day.

The body heat was only slightly mitigated by the open windows, letting in the tepid breeze of early October.

Liam managed to pace himself despite his roommates' encouragement to "*get fucked up, birthday boy!*" but he was pleasantly buzzed when a familiar face appeared in the doorway. He made an excited bleating noise that would have been embarrassing sober, clumsily toppling off Izzy's lap. Adjusting his skewed party hat, Liam slid in his socks across the wooden floor to greet Jonah.

"You're here!" he said. And maybe his alcohol tolerance wasn't as high as he thought, because he nearly lost his balance when he saw what Jonah was wearing. He decided not to bring direct attention to it, but Liam couldn't help but hook his finger in the familiar, tattered maroon sleeve at his wrist to pull him in.

They were getting better at this—the casual touching. Getting comfortable with it, though, didn't mean getting used to it. Liam's heart still jumped into his throat when Jonah surrendered easily to the invitation, twisting his hand to lace their fingers together.

"I'm here," Jonah agreed. With his free hand, he held up a lilac envelope. "Happy birthday."

A quiet beat passed between them, separate from the noise of the party. Jonah's eyes flicked to Liam's mouth. Liam answered the silent prompt by leaning forward and kissing him.

Something had shifted in the month since that day at the beach house. Neither Liam or Jonah ever took for granted the other's interest, always checking that the other was on board before doing anything sexual, but Liam knew they both felt the sizzling electricity between them when they shared a room. They'd spent several more nights together since, alternating between Liam's place and Jonah's.

Weekends were their haven. Between Friday night and Sunday evening, they were attached at the hip. During the days, they explored the city they were learning to call home, new neighborhoods each week, expanding their horizons to the places tourists didn't frequent. Jacob Riis Beach before the weather turned for the season, historic pizza shops in Gravesend, museums in the outer boroughs where Liam would study the art and Jonah would study Liam in his element.

On the wall above his bed, Liam had been collecting a montage of memories captured in a Polaroid camera he found at a thrift store. There was one of Jonah standing beneath the "Prince St." station mosaic subway tile sign. Another of Liam trying his first cigarette (and another of him hacking up a lung immediately after). His favorite was the photo of the two of them on Liam's living room floor, taken by Tucker the night Izzy convinced Liam to let her pierce his ear. Liam had one hand clutching a pillow and the other clutching Jonah, who looked at him like he was the brightest color in the world.

At night, they found new horizons in each other, inside darkened rooms, two explorers drawing their own map.

Tucker wolf-whistled from across the room, breaking apart their kiss. Jonah laughed and pressed the envelope into Liam's hands.

"Looks like I have some catching up to do." He lifted a hand to Liam's ear, just above his new piercing. "Can I get you another drink?"

Liam nodded, because it was hard to form words when Jonah was touching him like this, casual and affectionate and perfect. "I'd stay away from the concoction on the counter," he warned. "I think we accidentally made jet fuel."

Jonah glanced past him, toward the kitchen. "You mean the plastic tub of grey, opaque liquid? Yeah, I think I'll stick to something out of a bottle."

He departed with one last kiss to Liam's temple, waving a greeting to Liam's roommates on his way over.

Liam took the moment alone to carefully tear open the envelope, making sure not to damage any of its contents. The card he pulled out featured a cartoon dog from a children's show and big, bubble letters across the top that read *HAPPY 2nd BIRTHDAY*, with an extra *2* crammed in with marker. A laugh startled out of him, endlessly elated by these rare glimpses into Jonah's sense of humor, but it weaned to something softer when he opened the flap and saw the messy handwriting scrawled on the interior.

Liam,
Happy birthday.
Your boyfriend,
Jonah

Like a moth to flame, his eyes found Jonah's from across the room. His *boyfriend* paused halfway through opening a bottle at the kitchen counter, a slow, sheepish smile spreading across his face.

The party went on around them, oblivious to the strange, cosmic feeling of rightness that settled over Liam. Like this moment had been written in history long before they arrived at it. Like no matter how unlikely it might have seemed a year ago, they were always meant to find each other. They were exactly where they were meant to be, and happiness stretched out like an open road before them, theirs for the taking.

Liam closed the card and pressed it to his chest with gentle fingertips, hoping maybe Jonah felt it too.

■■■■■■■■■■■■■■■■■■■■■■■■■■■■■■■■■■■■■■■■■■■■■■■■■■■■

The party thinned out well after midnight.

Tucker barely made it past eleven before crushing Liam in a final happy birthday hug and stumbling off toward his bedroom. Izzy corralled their friends out of the apartment in search of a bar with an all-night kitchen. They'd invited Liam and Jonah, but it was a pretty clear formality. By that point in the night, there was no secrecy in their body language to hide the fact that they couldn't wait to be alone together.

Finally, when the living room was empty except for the mess of cups and bottles that would be tomorrow's problem, they got their wish.

Jonah had him pressed against the inside of his bedroom door, both hands cupping his jaw as he kissed him. His sweatshirt was already discarded in a heap on the floor, leaving his arms bare for Liam's exploration. It didn't take long before the kisses migrated to his neck. Liam let his head fall back against the wood. He was weightless and invincible in the afterglow of several glasses of cheap Prosecco, after a night of freedom and friendship and rare, selfish happiness.

But his mind was still clear enough to sense when Jonah's intentions shifted, his lips brushing the collar of his shirt, then trailing lower. Liam caught Jonah's sleeve before he could slip onto his knees, careful not to be forceful with his touch. Still, Jonah winced, a flicker of surprise giving way to confusion as he glanced up.

"Hey," Liam said, a little out of breath. "You don't have to do that tonight."

Jonah blinked. He studied Liam for a moment; cheeks pink from the alcohol and the heat between them. "You don't want me to?"

"I want *you*," Liam said, cupping Jonah's face, "to keep kissing me. Is that okay?"

Jonah searched his expression a moment longer, then granted Liam's request with enthusiasm.

Liam wasn't sure which of them made the first nudge toward the bed, or if their bodies were just in sync enough to feel the gravitational pull of it, but it wasn't long before they were stretched out on Liam's mattress, legs tangled and mouths moving.

Time was an indeterminable thing when they were like this. Liam was content to remain immersed in this magma-hot liquid euphoria forever. Jonah, as always, respected his wishes and kept his hands above Liam's waist, but even those touches—calloused hands splayed under his shirt, over his ribs, fingertips digging into his skin—were enough to light him from the inside out.

It was Liam who changed his mind, driven by the desire to show Jonah just how badly he wanted him back. He pulled back from the kiss, Jonah's teeth tugging at his bottom lip in a way that made his stomach flip, and asked, "Can I...?" He let his hand, trailing flat-palmed down the plane of Jonah's chest, finish the sentence for him.

The way they were intertwined, there was no missing the way Jonah's body tensed. He caught Liam's wrist too quickly to be casual.

"Wait." Then, as if catching his own reaction, Jonah schooled his expression into a shaky smile. It reminded Liam of the smile he used to see in the morning light shining through hotel curtains. The deflecting smile that tried hard to convince him that everything was okay when it wasn't.

"It's your birthday," Jonah said. "Shouldn't you be the center of attention tonight?"

Liam's mouth moved faster than his brain. "It's not just tonight, though."

Jonah pulled back an inch and went very, very still.

Liam cursed under his breath, because *shit*, he had not meant to say that out loud, and he hadn't meant to say it *like that*, and this was *not* a conversation to have while even partially intoxicated. But maybe the alcohol was to blame for the slip. Liam had been bottling this unease for weeks, and now, with his inhibitions lowered and emotions high, it was spilling out of him.

That day in the Long Island house had opened the floodgates on physical intimacy between them. Early mornings and late nights were stolen away in Jonah's room or Liam's, getting lost in the feeling of skin and breath and *love, love love*. It was everything Liam never knew he could want so much with another person.

But that joy didn't blind Liam to how one-sided things had been, physically.

Liam's inexperience meant Jonah was often the one taking the lead. Liam was more than happy to acquiesce to the guidance of his steady hands, but the result was an accumulation of memories of Jonah on his knees, Jonah with one hand down the front of Liam's shorts, Jonah gently catching Liam's wrist before things could venture too far toward reciprocity. It was too carefully curated to be anything but intentional, but still Liam held his tongue. Despite Jonah's claims to the contrary, Liam was never very good at finding the right words to talk about things, especially things that were this close to the heart, *this* important to get right.

So he had pushed down every real or perceived redirection in the dark, every thought that strayed too close to Jonah's past that Liam had no right to bring up, every itching thought in the back of his mind that told him there were some things that needed to be said out loud.

It wasn't meant to come out like this.

He probably should have stopped there, put a pin in this conversation until they were both clear-headed enough to talk about it with the care it deserved. But the look on Jonah's face told him he had opened a box that wouldn't easily close. Shutting it down now would only look like he was icing Jonah out.

"Sorry. That didn't come out right," Liam said. "I just worry sometimes that things are a little unbalanced between us. In that department."

Jonah's expression shuttered.

Liam was doing this all wrong, digging deeper with every word. *Stop talking. Stop talking. Stop talking.*

"Not that you need a reason to say no to something. You really don't. But I can't help but notice you've shot down all my attempts, and that's fine if you don't... You know, if you don't like to be touched like that. But I don't want to assume anything. I figured this was the kind of thing we should at least talk about."

A few moments passed in tense silence. Then, slowly, Jonah extracted himself from their tangle of limbs, leaving bitter cold in his absence. He pulled his knees to his chest, his back against the wall.

"I didn't realize you were so unhappy with what we've been doing." Jonah's voice was flat and toneless, a protective shell forming around him that Liam hadn't witnessed from him in so long that he almost didn't recognize it.

Liam wanted to eat his words, wanted to stuff them back down his throat and undo this whole conversation.

"You know I'm not," Liam said desperately, sitting up on his side of the bed, careful to keep their legs from touching. "Jonah, if that is genuinely just the way you like things—like, just giving instead of receiving—that's okay. I'm serious, you'll hear no complaints from me. But I never want to..." The words '*take advantage*' hit a little too close to Jonah's real history, so he swallowed him back. "I just think it would be good to know if that sort of thing is triggering for you."

Jonah's jaw tightened. He wouldn't meet Liam's eyes when he said, "I just know what I'm good at."

Liam put a hand to his stomach, steadying himself against the sudden, dizzy surge of nausea.

A whole lot of context was packed into so few words: that Jonah quantified his sexual prowess as *good* or *not good*, when so much of his experiences until now had been dubious at best and assault at worst.

A supercut of their most intimate encounters flashed before Liam, all tinged in a new, hideous light. How many of those times had Jonah just been falling back into old patterns? Had he ever forced himself through a sexual act for Liam's sake? He imagined Jonah closing his eyes, making his body numb to Liam's touch as he had with so many men before, and he wanted to throw up.

This whole time, Jonah had been carrying his demons into bed more than he ever let show, and Liam had been too caught to take proper notice.

Nathan's voice taunted him. *We're not so different after all, Cassidy.*

"I hate that you've been thinking about it in those terms," Liam whispered. "I hate that I've let you. I hate that you *ever* had to—" He scrubbed a palm over his mouth. "It's not about being *good*, Jonah. What you were forced to do before... it shouldn't feel like that with me. I don't *ever* want it to be that way with me."

"I'm trying my best."

Liam had hoped that his days of getting eviscerated by the drive by devastation of Jonah's words were behind him. It was so easy to get swept up in the progress they'd made, in the newfound light in Jonah's eyes and the rose-colored glasses of being in love for the first time. This was a sobering reminder of just how steep a mountain Jonah was climbing, even on the days he didn't let his struggle show.

Liam had taken up that post at his side willingly, *happily*, but now he felt like he had failed him.

Jonah was the picture of misery, shoulders curled in and fingers pressed to his eyelids, looking like he wanted the world to disappear around him.

"Listen," Liam said. "I've been doing some reading. Online. There are these... They're not quite support groups, just like, community forums I guess. For the partners of victims of..." The word shriveled in the back of his throat. "People who have a history with sexual trauma."

The air in the room went stagnant and stale.

"I haven't said anything about you," Liam rushed to assure him. "I promise. I've just been reading other people's stories, trying to find some sort of... guidance."

"'*Victim.*'" Worse than Jonah's silence was the cold non-inflection in his voice as he repeated Liam's poor word choice back at him. "Is that what you see when you look at me?"

"No. Jonah, *no–*" Horror cut him short, a knot forming tight in his stomach.

Denial was an easy, knee-jerk reaction, and he was sure he meant it as he said it, but Jonah's words planted a seed of doubt. *Was* that what Liam saw when he looked at Jonah? Even a little? Even without meaning to? From the very first night they met, Liam had been conscious of the dynamic between them and tried to navigate carefully. Their circumstances were different now, but that didn't erase the truth of their history, which was that Jonah *had* been victimized, and Liam had borne witness to his suffering in a way he couldn't forget.

That didn't change the love he had for Jonah, not then and not now. But something must have shown in Liam's expression, twisting Jonah's thoughts into the worst assumption, because he lurched forward quick enough to make Liam jump, all knees and elbows as he clambered off the mattress, stumbling several feet across the hardwood.

"I need some air," Jonah said, stuffing his bare feet into his shoes.

Liam followed after him, rising from the bed with palms raised. They'd been here before, too: Jonah and his instinct to run when he felt the walls closing in, and Liam desperate to show him that he was a safe place to stay.

"Jonah," he said gently, reaching out to steady him.

Jonah flinched.

He flinched *away from Liam.*

If the air had gone stagnant before, it vacated the room entirely now. Liam's hand dropped to his side, deadweight. Jonah met his eyes for the first time since the start of the doomed conversation. They were bloodshot and exhausted, skin blotched pink at the corners. He stole his gaze away as quickly as he'd granted it.

"I'm sorry," he said.

Before Liam could find the words to reply, Jonah bolted from the room.

▪▪▪▪▪▪▪▪▪▪▪▪▪▪▪▪▪▪▪▪▪▪▪▪▪▪▪▪▪▪▪▪▪▪▪▪▪▪▪▪▪▪▪▪▪▪▪▪

Liam tried to give him space, at first.

He made it ten minutes before peeking over the side of the fire escape.

He made it twenty minutes before climbing up to the technically-off-limits rooftop they'd made out on once.

Jonah was nowhere to be found.

The last of Liam's restraint caved ten minutes after that, when he sent Jonah a text only to watch his phone light up from the top of the dresser.

He'd left it behind.

The writhing panic in his gut was probably, mostly irrational. Jonah was a grown man, and plenty of people have existed in this city without a cell phone and lived to tell the tale.

That didn't stop Liam from reaching for his shoes at two in the morning and stepping out into the October night.

By the time he stepped out of the train station in Forest Hills, it had started to rain. Liam was soaked by the time he stepped onto the porch of the old house, sneakers squashing wetly under each step and hair plastered to his head.

He gave little consideration to the neighbors as he knocked, then pounded, on the door. He paused to listen for signs of movement on the other side, wrapping his arms around himself to stave off the cold. When he raised his hand to knock again, the door swung open, revealing Antonio Ellis, looking surprisingly un-rumpled by sleep and grasping at something at the back of his waistband the way someone might reach for a service weapon. Liam took a step back, but Ellis pulled his hand away when he took in the young man on his doorstep.

"Liam?"

"Is Jonah here?" he asked, loud enough to be heard over the pounding of rain on the porch roof.

"I thought he was with you. What happened?"

It sounded a little too much like he meant to say *what did you do?* and Liam didn't appreciate the accusation. As if this fucker had any room to play at protectiveness.

"Did he come back here or not?" he snapped, probably with all the ferocity of a shivering chihuahua, given his current state.

"Only for a minute. He asked if he could borrow the truck."

"And you let him?" Jonah hadn't really had that much to drink, so the train ride back to Queens was probably more than enough to sober him up, but Liam wasn't much in the mood for logic right now.

"Why wouldn't I?" Ellis said. "He said he needed some room to breathe. I figured that was better than going for a walk." He gave a pointed look to Liam's soggy form. "For obvious reasons."

"Did he say where he was going?" Liam asked. But even as the words left his mouth, the answer clicked into place.

The memory of salty sea air, wind-blown curls, and smudges of pastel on bronze skin. *"It feels like you can breathe easier out here."*

"Look," Ellis said. "Do you want to come in and dry off before we have this conversation?"

"No," Liam said, already reaching for the half-waterlogged phone in his pocket. "I think I know where he is. I'm calling a car."

"Call it in here, where it's warm," Ellis insisted. "And let me give you my number. Please, let me know that he's safe."

■■■■■■■■■■■■■■■■■■■■■■■■■■■■■■■■■■■■■■■■■■■■■■■■■■

It took an upfront tip of fifty-percent to convince the driver to let him into the backseat dripping in rainwater. For once, Liam allowed himself to feel less sleazy for accepting the small allowance his parents dropped into his bank account once a month.

The grandiose Long Island McMansion came into view like something out of a gothic horror, the only house on the street without lights glaring up at it from the garden. Jonah had told him that the house sat empty for most of the year, but especially while the renovations finished through the fall.

If Liam was wrong about this, he was probably risking a 911 call from a concerned neighborhood watch about a suspicious, wet man loitering in a neighborhood outside his tax bracket. It would also mean he was out of ideas for where to find Jonah, and that was arguably the worse consequence.

But when the car pulled up in front of the house, Liam could make out the vague shape of Ellis's truck in the dark driveway. His chest deflated with relief.

Liam shot the driver a wave and a thank you as he closed the door behind him, wincing at the puddle he left behind on the leather seat. Now, at least, the rain had slowed to a faint drizzle as he made his way up the driveway.

The front door had keyless entry. Liam thanked whatever cosmic entity had compelled him to watch Jonah enter the five-digit code on the keypad previously. It only took a couple failed attempts before Liam got the green light.

There was probably a time in his life where he would have cared more about unlawfully entering someone's home, but that time was not today.

His footsteps echoed inside the half-empty house, damp prints trailing in his wake. Sparing a thought for the homeowners, he slipped his shoes off at the edge of the foyer, but the rain had already soaked down to his socks.

"Jonah?" he called out at the base of the staircase. He wanted to avoid startling him, if he hadn't already heard the door open and shut.

After a moment of tense, weighted silence, he heard, "Liam?"

Liam released a breath. He bounded up the stairs two at a time, catching himself on the railing as his wet socks slid on marble. In the second floor hallway, he turned and found Jonah in the open glass doorway of the terrace off the primary bedroom. The hard line of his shoulders rose toward his ears, his arms wrapped around himself like a shield. It was the silhouette of a man braced for a storm—one Liam had no intention of bringing.

"Hi," Liam said softly.

"How did you know I was here?" It was hard to make out Jonah's expression in the dark, but he could tell from his voice that he had been crying. Liam tried not to let the thought kneecap him where he stood.

"A lucky guess, a train ride, a waterlogged car, and a quick pit stop in Queens," Liam said. "Not necessarily in that order."

Jonah's eyes traveled over him as Liam stepped out of the darkness of the hall and into the moonlight-drenched room. "You're wet."

"Yeah," Liam agreed.

"You came after me." Jonah said it like he couldn't quite believe the words himself. "All this way, in the middle of the night. In the rain."

"Of course I did." As if there was any version of reality where Liam simply rolled over and went to sleep in a bed Jonah had fled from. As if Liam wouldn't have crossed far more than a few bridges and tunnels to find him.

"I left you," Jonah insisted. "On your birthday."

"I don't care about that."

"You should." Jonah's expression darkened. "You should be angry at me. You deserve better than that." The unspoken words rang just as loud in the empty house: *You deserve better than me.*

Liam took a step closer, slow in his approach. "You're the one who taught me that first, you know," he said. "That I deserve better. You're also the one who showed me what *better* looks like."

Jonah turned his head away, a thin glow of moonlight tracing the strong line of his nose. He didn't have anything to say to that, so Liam went on.

"What you said back there... You asked if I saw a victim when I looked at you. Is that really what you think?"

"Maybe that's all that I am." Jonah's voice, low and gravelly, was nearly stolen away by the wind off the ocean at his back. "We can't pretend I'm someone different now. A piece of me is always going to be stuck back there. I'm always going to be that boy in the hotel room, in my memory and in yours."

Liam moved closer. "You're right about one thing," he allowed. "I *will* always remember the boy from that hotel room, and all the ones that came after. Because that boy turned my entire world upside down."

He made it to the threshold of the glass sliding door and stopped, leaving them on opposite sides of the opening. Liam was close enough now to make out the twitch in Jonah's jaw, a clear tell that he teetered on the fault line of warring emotions.

"You're right about another thing," Liam continued. "You *are* the same person you were then. And when I look at you, Jonah, I don't just see a collection of your saddest stories. You're so much more than that, and you always have been." Liam so badly wanted to take his face between his palms, to make him see the truth staring back at him, but he kept his distance. "Even when you were in that horrible place, the things that happened to you were never who you were. I wasn't drawn to your circumstances, but I didn't run from them, either. It was always just about being close to *you*."

Jonah finally looked at him, and his expression shattered on impact. Tears cut down his cheeks, catching at his jawline. "You're the only one who ever deserved any part of me," Jonah said. "And now I don't have anything left to give. What if they took it all before I met you?"

"They didn't," Liam whispered. "You're still here. You survived despite them all. That's what matters."

"Liam, come *on*." Jonah dragged a hand through his hair. "How long can you keep writing this off? You've always been too nice to me, but eventually even *you* will reach a limit. It's been a year since we met. A *year*, and I'm still falling apart. I was happy tonight. *We were happy*, and then I was losing my shit and running away, and it's like nothing ever—" He cut a singular, sharp shake of his head, like the matter was decided. "You deserve to be with someone who doesn't freak the fuck out when you try to touch him."

"I don't want them," Liam shot back. "Whatever hypothetical person, whatever alternate reality you've created for me in your head where you think I would be so much happier, I *don't want it*. I want *you*. I know exactly what I signed up for, and nothing has changed on that front."

"It could," Jonah said. "It might. You say you're fine with it now, but what if one day you wake up and realize you've changed your mind. I've lost so much in the last few years. I don't think I could stand losing you and knowing it was all my fault."

Liam finally breached the doorway, planting both feet on the terrace, only inches left between them.

"None of this," he said, "is your fault."

He held out a hand, and after a moment, Jonah took it, staring down at where their skin touched like it was something from a dream.

"I want this," Jonah said. A tear ran to the tip of his nose and clung on. "I want this with you so badly."

"You have it," Liam promised. "I *love* you, Jonah. I'm not going anywhere."

Jonah's breath escaped him in a sob. Liam was close enough to catch him when he crumbled. He crushed Jonah against him, and Jonah clung on with everything he had left, finally letting Liam take some of his weight.

If Jonah deserved everything, the whole experience, flowers and chivalry and all, then he deserved this too: someone who would cross the city in the rain for a tear-soaked declaration of love.

They had loved each other for so long now without needing to speak the words. The things they'd done for each other, the gentle handling of each other's hearts, had always spoken louder. But tonight, there was power in saying it out loud.

"I love you," Liam repeated, Jonah's soft hair brushing his lips. He kissed his head, felt his body shaking against him, and said it again. "I love you."

They stayed like that long enough for the rain to transfer from Liam's clothes to Jonah's, leaving both of them damp and shivering but warm where their bodies touched. Liam made himself remember every sensory detail of this moment. Jonah's breath tickling his neck, the weight of him against Liam's body, the ripple of the water behind the house.

When they finally pulled apart, Jonah's tears had dried, but the toll this night had taken was evident in the lines of his face.

They borrowed a couple of old zip-ups from Ellis's truck and brought them back upstairs—they'd already done the breaking and entering, they might as well stick around for the sunrise. They peeled out of their wet shirts in silence, just the whisper of fabric and the spread of goosebumps across naked, moonlit skin. There was something intimate about it; not touching but not looking away either. No room for shyness or shame in all the love between them.

At the first smudge of bronze light on the horizon, they sat on the terrace, side by side. They watched the glow spread across the sky in perfect silence, hands linked on top of Jonah's thigh. When the sun was high enough to chase the shadow on the terrace up to their ankles, Liam dared to break the silence.

"You don't ever have to run when it comes to me." He rolled his head to the side so he could study Jonah in profile. "If you ever feel like you did tonight, please don't go. Stay with me. Let me help you figure it out."

After a moment, Jonah nodded. He dropped his gaze on their joined hands, running a free fingertip over the prominent vein in Liam's wrist. "I think I'm going to look for a therapist," he said.

Words were pedestrian in the wake of an admission like this. Instead, Liam wrapped a careful arm around

Jonah's shoulders and pulled him close once more, burying his lips in the nest of his hair.

Exhaustion crept in. Sleepless nights were a familiar thing between them. They had built the foundation of their relationship on them once upon a time, and Liam would weather a thousand more if that was what it meant to have a permanent place at Jonah's side.

As the morning settled over them, Jonah's body went limp against Liam's, sleep finally pulling him under.

"Lean on me," Liam whispered. "I can handle it."

# CHAPTER 10
# Jonah

Fridays had a new routine these days.

Jonah rose before the sun, but it wasn't to pull on his work clothes, as he had become so accustomed to doing since the beginning of last summer. In the dead of an ice-cold March, the construction gigs had slowed down. There were less open spots on the crew for the projects they got, and Jonah had been the first to volunteer to take a step back. His life was changing, and for once, that transitionary period felt less like stepping off a cliff into darkness and more like taking hold of the reins for the very first time.

He crossed paths with Ellis in the kitchen, who had saved a cup of coffee for Jonah and blearily sipped his own against the counter. They exchanged a murmured *"morning"* as Jonah went about making his toast.

"Can I drop you at the train?" Ellis asked.

"I'm okay to walk. Thanks." There was something cleansing about the cold in New York City. On Friday mornings, Jonah craved that grounding force more than usual.

He looked over at the sudden *schlick* of paper across the countertop and found an envelope beneath Ellis's fingertips, presented to him without commentary. The formal university logo on the return address made Jonah's heart skip. He met Ellis's eyes, carefully blank and unassuming, then pulled the letter toward himself.

A month from now, Jonah would hit his one-year mark as a New York resident. By the fall semester, he would be eligible for free tuition at the CUNY colleges—a scholarship opportunity he hadn't known about until Ellis introduced him.

"I'll open it later," Jonah said.

Ellis waited until Jonah's back was to him, rinsing his plate at the sink. "Whatever that letter says," he said in a low voice, "and whatever you decide to do with it, I'm proud of you."

Jonah's hands faltered a moment. He let the words sink into him.

Ellis was not his father. With their dubious history, he would never quite hit the mark of a father *figure*. But in the absence of Jonah's parents in his life, it was nice to hear someone—not just *anyone*, but someone who had witnessed more of his suffering and his treacherous climb up from the bottom than anyone else alive—say it out loud.

■■■■■■■■■■■■■■■■■■■■■■■■■■■■■■■■■■■■■■■■■■■■■■■■■■■■■

His therapist's office was located in a high-rise building in Long Island City. Jonathan had a welcoming space with a retro-futuristic sofa in the shape of a bean, a pride flag posted on the door, and a well-groomed shih tzu named Carl's Jr. He had a terrible underbite and an affinity for ramming his head into Jonah's ankles when he wasn't getting enough attention. (Carl's Jr., not Jonathan).

Jonah had cried more within those walls in the last four months than he had in his entire life. However difficult he had anticipated it would be to air out his past, to lay everything out in the open where he could no longer look away from it, the reality was even harsher.

He had chosen Jonathan, after weeks of consideration, partly because of his openness about his own past: he was a transgender man from the bible belt of the American South. His website said he specialized in PTSD from abuse and sexual assault. Jonah was coming to terms with applying those labels to the things he had survived. It was too easy sometimes to look back and only see the string of his own mistakes that had run his life off course. Jonathan liked to remind him that laying blame did not make for an easy road forward, especially when it was all piled onto himself.

When he broke it down, these were the facts: Jonah was a kid when his parents turned their backs on him. He was barely legal when Dominic took an interest. He was powerless by the time Ross Shepard had him in his grip. He had never been asking for it. What happened to Jonah, as Liam had begged him to believe, was never his fault.

But that didn't mean he wouldn't be the one to carry it for the rest of his life.

"It isn't fair," Jonathan had told him. "And it isn't kind. But the hurt that sticks with us doesn't have to be the thing that defines us. It doesn't get to control your life anymore, Jonah."

Most days, Jonah actually believed him.

"I let Liam touch me," he announced on this particular Friday.

Jonathan's brows lifted behind the wall of steam rising from his cup—something herbal and minty he always kept on hand for his sessions.

The phrasing was an oversimplification. It wasn't as if Jonah was shy about the terminology. He didn't have that in him anymore. But it was a criminal mischaracterization to call what Liam had done for him by the same name as his own lived experience. *Blowjob* was too crass a word to describe the way Liam had come to him slowly, bringing Jonah's fingers to his mouth to show his intent. Waiting until Jonah's eyes were heavy-lidded, his breathing labored, before moving elsewhere. Placing a grounding hand flat on Jonah's abdomen and a kiss to his hip bone.

Liam had approached the act with a singular focus that implied a level of preparative research, which was so quintessentially *Liam* that Jonah couldn't help but find comfort in it.

It wasn't the first time they'd attempted reciprocation after the night of Liam's birthday, but it was the first time they'd gotten through the encounter without Jonah having to end things prematurely. In all the times Jonah had to tell him to stop, Liam never got angry. Slowly, Jonah was learning to stop bracing for it. Even more slowly, he was learning not to be so angry at *himself.*

Both Jonathan and Liam liked to remind him that *"real sex"* wasn't defined by any one act, and that what they had done so far could be all there was to it, if that was what they wanted. Jonah didn't know if that was what he wanted or not—or if he could even handle *more*—but having the space to decide for himself made all the difference. It was more than Jonah ever thought he would get to have again.

For a year of his life, Jonah's world had been isolated to a series of small, dark spaces. Basements and backseats and hotel rooms where the sun couldn't reach him. Those places would always exist somewhere in his memory, and there would be bad days when he stumbled into them, getting caught up in the feeling of walls closing in around him. But those walls couldn't hold him anymore. Now, Jonah was free to kick open the doors, throw open the windows, and let the light in.

There was a lot more light in Jonah's life these days. One particularly bright beam waited for him on the park bench outside the office when his session ended, nose and cheeks pink from the chill. It was a routine he had come to rely on: a warm cup of coffee from the corner store waiting for him, a brush of fingers against his own on the days he could handle the contact, or a quiet presence at his side on the days he couldn't. It never mattered where they went or what they did. Jonah had fallen in love with Liam in the darkest of waters, clinging to the last beam of light on the horizon. Now his feet were planted on the shore, and possibility sprawled before him.

Liam looked up as Jonah approached, his smile coming to life.

The darkness didn't stand a chance.

# ACKNOWLEDGMENTS

After I published my debut novel at the end of last year, it became clear very quickly that these two characters weren't finished with me yet.

As I sat down to figure out what came next for me, Liam & Jonah were there every step of the way, whispering in my ear about all the moments they never got to play out in their happily-ever-after. There was so much left to explore in New York, and if I was going to spend all my time thinking about them, I might as well share those ideas with the readers who had expressed interest in reading more.

Some much-deserved thanks:

To everyone who loved Liam & Jonah enough to seek out more of their story. You've made my author dreams come true.

To Jessica Sherburn for the beautiful cover art. I'm so very grateful to now have a matching set of book covers in your style.

To Cara & Marie, my beta readers who have supported Liam & Jonah's story since the beginning and gave me such valuable feedback on the novella.

To Jonathan Hawker for offering your perspective and encouragement as a sensitivity reader.

To Melyn McHenry for coming in to polish up the last round of edits.

To my dad for picking up his first book since high school in order to read *A Series of Rooms* last year.

To whatever stranger currently resides in my first New York City apartment. You might recognize my description of Liam's place. Say hi to the mice for me.

And to my partner. Writing can be such lonely work. You make it better.